The Cauldron of Hope

Abhinav Bhattacharyya

©

ISBN: 978-93-5406-922-2

DEDICATION

To Priyanka, Anubhav, Mom, Dad, Aunt Amy, and a tribute to the
two Legends who made this happen.

May our tryst with Hope and History stay ignited forever!

Map of the High Seas

ACKNOWLEDGMENTS

Special mention to Priyanka Adhikary (My Wife) and Anubhav Bhattacharyya (Brother) for their extraordinary support and motivation, otherwise the book would have been lost in transition, like a bunch of illegible doctors prescriptions in a dull folder.

A bow to two of my best friends "The Captain" (Amit Sahu) and "The Criminal" (Alok Gupta), on whom I love to relate the two prime characters of my work. The latter is missing in action, so anyone reading this book, please notify the Author i.e. ME, if you happen to find his whereabouts.

Mom, Dad, and Dear Aunt (Amy), thanks for the never-ending excitement for the cause, even when I was stuck in Chapter 1 for long. I hope you like the book and please do skip the areas where there is any mention of adultery or incest.

Finally, I would like to add a special vote of thanks to my dear friend and ex-roomie John (Chigozie Obioma). Without his literary directions and insightful tips, it would have been quite difficult to complete my work with quality.

CONTENTS

PROLOGUE

8

" The atmosphere was still, so was the druid. He strongly believed in his rare art of healing and his prowess in herbal medicine.

A man lay before him, clad in a piece of fine white silk. A Mild fever had bestowed upon his mortal soul. In deep tranquil was he, intoxicated by the strong antidote infused upon him by the grandmaster of remedy. Soon utopia beckoned..... "

"I have seen far and wide, even the beyond,

Have fought in many wars and won them all.

Respect, camaraderie, love and friendship, I earned them all,

The earth, them seas, the air, I have it all!

I worry and pray, it continues on, well after my days are gone.

There is only one thing I wish, I dream on, tis Hope and that's all."

---------- Unknown verses of a known Legend.

1. THE KINGDOM OF THE HOPELESS

"He was soaring, high up in them clear blue skies. The druid tending to him now formed into a fat little angel. The angel was saying something to him, he crept near from cloud to cloud. Soon a voice rang in his ears, a voice pristine yet filled with solace. It spoke and for long.........................

Once upon a time in a land very near, there lived a king, a captain and a criminal. Of course, along with other un-characteristic beings; but describing them at length would make the story considerably dull. Until a very wet day their paths never crossed and the land was devoid of irony or even its existence.

The king was young but he acted old. Always in a drunken stupor, in the glittering gold of the day and the dusky ivory of the night. Taxes were high, citizen poor. Produce was good but substantial grains were subject to mortgages for daily needs. The royal treasury was an assortment of gold, grains and other gains. Gold primarily from sea excursions and loot of petty merchant ships laden with the same.

The captain was a connoisseur of the seas. A Perfectionist in pirate maneuvers and an expert executioner of deep-sea looting expeditions. Fueled by rum, driven by his insane imagination he kept the royal treasury well stocked with gold and gains. He was the supreme authority of the high seas for the kingdom but whence inland a mere petty citizen. Even the king didn't recognize his exploits since he was rather busy drowning in his ocean of liquor. The captain was extremely cheerful when in the sea than rather inland and often cursed "in-land" beings. "Downtrodden Mongrels" who are the protectors of the "Scum King" he stated often. Fellow seamen in his vessel often overheard him blabber all day long about the "kingdom of doom". That's what he called the land.

The law of the land; the king was an icon of lawlessness. Rather named by petty citizens "the bacchanal king", "the mad king", "the blind one", "dead meat", "the goner". But none of the wraths even made it to his ears or his courtroom. His ministers were meticulously keeping him happy with the booze and the fresh meat; in turn, keeping their pockets brimming with gold pieces offered by *his 'boozing grace'* as rewards for information and public service.

The army, a mere dozen armed guards, rather guarding the royal treasury were the only honest citizens; because if not this job which paid them a living stipend, there was nothing better to explore. The markets were regulated by the ministers and taxes too. Inflation reaching new heights. Forging the royal order to declare double taxation to keep both the king at bay and their pockets booming. Theft amongst the population was common, including murder for food and other necessities.

The courtroom had been completely upturned to match a "carny amphitheater" the "room of lust", where jewels laden naked femme dancers entertained the 'mad king'. Wine & hops poured into glasses all day long also drenched the extravagant carpets. Lavish chandeliers, glittering royal gold ware, embroidered walls of mosaic and massive art pieces encompassed the nonliving part of the giant hall.

"The fool's happy and so are we", a minister said to the other brimming with divine confidence and a nasty smirk. Growling loudly said the other lord "Long live the king, the messiah of the land". Acknowledged by a few coins of gold thrown at him the king thundered "Noble thoughts keep them flowing". Throwing the empty glass on the rich floor, he ordered a courtesan to get it filled to the brim. Exotic dancers and their stamping and thumping along with the loud orchestra flowing out from the musical instruments created a humongous uproar which resonated beyond the end of the "kingdom of doom".

There was only one man in the kingdom who labeled the land on a rather positive note "the cauldron of hope". That would most certainly be the criminal.

--------------------------------------XXXXXXXXXXXXXXX--

2. The Captain

The voice went on, it rang in his ears aloud .... "A leader of a pack, a master of a group, a commander of them soldiers and finally a seaborne captain has many things similar. Except at sea the master seafarer plays multiple roles. Sometimes a father, at times a brother, once a leader and then a friend. But most importantly his decisions has to be perfectly aligned, a thread outside them boundaries is but uncertainty. Bad weather and pirates adore uncertainty, which finally leads to low confidence and to top it all, death. A death without a funeral at times, not celebrated nor attended by many, escape is as good as hope. Hope is a fairy who teases many at sea. So does our captain, he too is bitten rarely by hope and the dreaded melancholy."

With thunderous laughter and a bottle half-filled with rum the prodigal son of the high sea fell into it. Trout and snappers splashing out of the drop zone. Spools of fish avoiding the interaction with the gaffer of the high seas. "Make way for the conqueror of a thousand ships, the gold mountain, the slayer of the wrong; the protector of the right, the undisputed ruler of the sacred seas; The Captain" lambasted one of his favorite seamen. Popping his head out of the mighty sea the captain thundered "I pray, do you remember the last time we were ever defeated at sea my friend". "Ha Ha Ha Ha dare not anyone rubs us on the wrong side when the mighty captain is alive and kicking," said the favorite seamen in a pompous note. "Seventeen days sea bound we are, can smell gold only today; Ha Ha Ha Ha, let's follow the sacred scent my boy" glared the captain.

His laughter still echoing several miles into the high seas. "O governor of the seas, your word is our command" stated the favorite seamen. "Pull me up to my beast" uttered the captain referring to his lead vessel. Bright sunny skies, sharp blue in color, a horizon filled with his fleet of seven raiding ships, ready to pounce upon his command and the infinite waters of the high seas.

"Ahoy, full speed ahead" glared the mighty captain. Back on the dry wooden deck the captain booming with divine confidence and his signature smile strolled towards his afternoon spot. His mahogany desk awaited him, well cut and dried out of a single piece of the finest wood. His lunch was served, a wholesome trout marinated with salt and pepper; smoked for the ample hour. He cracked open a bottle of hos divine sprit the rum, which he personally encroached from a merchant ship of the far lands during a remarkable conquest in the sea. Glittering his teeth were, of gold; smiling end to end was he, devouring his moment of joy in the high-sea.

After consuming his feisty meal, he stood for a full view of the sea route ahead. Slowly drowning in his plethora of thoughts he sighed. Dark was his skin, sun-dried; taller than a ladder, with a well-oiled physique. He glared at the sun and the approaching blast of wind, for he was recognized and acknowledged by them. "With having my fleet and the well-seasoned experience of valor, the wrecked ships, the loot, the hills of gold; should I be happier thee; tell me my lord" expressed the captain looking towards the blue skies. Suddenly the sky went gloomy and the clouds wept. Showers of tear bestowed down on him and he felt them droplets ensemble on his face. The brightness left the darkness arrived. The wind called upon his rowdy brother, the storm into persistence.

"Why does he not understand, I am the root cause of his existence, his royal treasure is defined by my triumph at sea" he muttered with a reference to the mad king. "After making him richer than any king or their kingdom, he treats me as if I am the bane of his sole existence; he makes me talk to his conniving hands in the ministry, who treats me like a novice fisherman" uttered the captain in a dejected note.

Gloom came down from the skies along with the thunder of the gods in acknowledgment of the mighty captain's remorse. Dusk engulfed the great mind and the great man stated, "Why should I fear that bacchanal king, he who never understood revenue and stability of his kingdom of doom". "Why do I continue to usurp the wealth of many to the king feet, when the glory is unaccounted for and never recognized."

Creeping behind the masquerader of the seas and grabbing him with utmost stealth his favorite seaman muttered, "Why the gloom my dear captain, thee shall see victory soon". Immediately booming in divine confidence, the mighty captain retorted "Yes, we shall raid soon, I can smell the variance of the salts in the winds". "I am telling you, it's a merchant ship laden with glitter to the brim, destined for the far lands" the captain mentioned in an excited tone. "Unfortunately, destiny in the high seas is designed and directed by me" glared the captain and let out a stupendous laugh which echoed infinite miles. "Ahoy captain, do you hear it, lads, let's be sharper tomorrow morning because the fate is designated and thee has given his worldly direction" glared the favorite seaman to his fellow mates on deck.

Soon the moon shone in the starry skies and dusk prevailed the air, but the water glittered, so did the massive mast of the lead vessel by the reflections of the light of the moon god, the protector of the night sea. The captain strolled down to the deck to be welcomed by the panoramic view of the massive mast glazing in the divine congregation of light bestowed by the moon and the stars; it stood still in the gale force, undermining all forces of nature. In the profound melodrama of the situation the captain rolled down his thoughts, "Oh beautiful sea, the lord of water; let me have a longer steak and pompous gains this time around".

Out of the flickering stars flying with great urgency in came a hiero-falcon stooping towards his master. "oh, my eyes, my heart, my soul, my dearest friend, welcome back the grandmaster of the high seas" the captain lambasted, extending his hand for his pet to rest. "Great falcon, the lord of the birds, the messenger of the sea; what news do you behold for me," the captain asked the hiero-falcon patting him as he spoke. The great falcon flew slightly right of the mast, rested on the boundary and hooted out loud. "O my dear friend, you saw the prey, to the northeast of our position" glared the captain. "Oh, you intelligent being, how many a times you have brought grand news to thee" exclaimed the captain in a pompous mood.

The grand falcon flew back to its master's arm to rest. "Ahoy, all men on deck, hear me out, set sail northeast, we shall soon see glory there" commanded the master of the high seas. An amalgamated thunderous response resounded, "Aye Aye captain, northeast it is". The message was relayed to the other raiding ships in his fleet and acknowledged with flickering lights of a seaman's lamp, in Morse-code famous in the high seas. The captain petted his hiero-falcon and retired from the deck to his cabin to rest for the night.

The dawn bestowed upon the high seas, a poly chromatic effervescence of the presence of the sun god. Bright rays of the lord of light rested upon the eyelids of the captain, penetrating the windowsills in its path. A weary captain, hungover by the foregone nights exploits woke up. "Oh, lord of lights, Oye my great falcon; am I late for the grand occasion", muttered the captain. The great messenger of the high seas flew from his restive spot to land in his old friends' chest. "Haste is it, my dear friend; then haste it shall be" exclaimed the captain. Dashing on to the deck, the captain glared "Oye, someone get me a periscope". With great urgency his favorite seaman got him his second favorite set of eyes.

The captain concentrated on finding his desired score in the seas, moved from end to end of his divine carrier. Alas, when he directed his vision ahead, standing at the very end of the falcon's head of his galley, did he see a shape in the sea. "Oh, my man, did I see something of interest" exclaimed the captain with excitement and hope. The favorite seaman glared through his eyepiece and suddenly after a while of observation; his expression changed to that of a schoolboy who had seen a fruitcake. "By thee, my great lord, the guvnor of the high seas; it is a ship, rather a merchant ship, my lord". With a humongous laughter the captain thundered "let us lay a trap to make thy enemy comfortable, I command all ships to lower their mast, the entire fleet to maintain a broad line, all seamen to dress like fishermen with fishnets hanging from the deck and cover all falcon heads of the prow of the ships with dirty linen to make I look real".

Seamen hustled to fulfill the sea rulers command, relaying messages were acknowledged immediately by the entire fleet. The fleet of raiding ships fell into a broad line, resembling a fishing excursion. Men aboard dressed and acted like able-fishermen of the high seas. Humongous nets were in place to match the ploy. The scene was set, the captain too appeared in a torn fisherman pants along with a coned hat to mark the beginning of a very detailed act to lure the gold.

After an hour the merchant ship, now very clear from the mast; rather from the kingdom of the far-lands; approached the fleet without a morsel of doubt. The mighty captain, the conniving conqueror of the sea let out a murky smile and stated " HA HA HA HA finally the big fish has responded; make no haste my good men, be alert and keep your swords and cutlass ready; we shall pounce at once they are at arm's length. A conjunction of nods acknowledged his grace, the able captain of their confidence in the state of affairs.

Soon the merchant ship neared the lead vessel and a pompous looking merchant glared "Oye, we are the great merchants and the forbearer of the wealth of the ruler of the kingdom of the far-lands". "We shall trade a few shoals of fish for gold coins; how was the day's catch of your men?" questioned the pompous merchant of the far-lands. The captain resounded with an aura of approval "Ahoy, the great lords of the far-lands, it's a pleasure to do business with you any day, your tales of justice and business proficiency is known all across the near lands and also by the sea laden". "Kindly pray thee to fasten ships so that we can help make the deal a successful escapade" stated the captain. Shouting a few fake orders to display an urgency for the upcoming business, the captain ordered his able seamen to drop anchor across the merchant ship to lock them together. Without any air of resentment, the seamen of the merchant ship followed the same. The captain drew his sword slowly towards his hand and grabbed it without displaying the blade. He then took a deep breath and smiled towards the falcon then at his men. His men nodded in acknowledgment. The stage has been set and a final command awaited the massacre.

The captain of the high seas, the protector of the kingdom of doom, glarèd louder than the loudest voice ever heard "Ahoy, attack them with brute force". All seamen along with the captain jumped onboard the deck of the merchant ship. In utter shock and dismay the petty merchants tried to flee. Defenseless they were, the merchants of the far lands when flashing blades rained upon them. Blood flowing freely like a river on deck, cries and prayers for mercy fell in deaf ears. The falcon too had found a prey; snatching an eye of a merchant trying to defend his honor. After a brisk few minutes there were only a couple of merchants left bruised but alive.

A broad smile bestowed on the captain's deep cut face. Soon the day's glory, the loot of gold and other gains were amassed on the deck. "Count these guineas and bars, assemble all gains and carry it overboard to my vessel' ordered the captain. He looked upon the live ones and smiled. Then slowly his mood changed as one of the merchants made a bold statement. "I failed to honor my lord of the far-lands and also thee, the great ruler of the high seas, out of sheer ignorance of my own'. "May I, a feeble human as for an honorable death by a duel with thy lord". All seamen pleaded the captain to fight, convinced of the victory; out dull and rare foolish entertainment. But this time the captain in retrospect glared "Never have I ever not slaughtered merchants of the far lands and other Vikings in the sea; but I also do not hold you a coward or a fool for not recognizing me". You and your mate shall sail in a gondola back to your far lands and tell the tale of the massacre at sea to your king and the population". "You are free, my dear merchant, my wise friend" exclaimed the captain.

In utter shock, a serene silence spread across the sea, the birds flew near without chirping, the able seamen of the grand fleet stood like mere statues, the merchant too was frozen in awe. "Oye, my friend" glared the captain to his favorite seaman and declared "lend my dear merchant friend a gondola". With utter dismay the seaman lowered a boat into the high seas. The captain held the speechless merchant along with his fellow seaman and helped them down to their fate.

Finally out of great honor and faith the merchant shouted: "O my lord, have I ever seen a kinder soul than thee, nay, all stories of wrath of yours are untrue by this very moment, I shall speak of you for years to come, my dear captain, the messiah of the high seas". "I plead my lord, I owe you my life, I shall repay you one day with life only". Saying that the two sole survivors of the far-lands set sail towards their promised land.

Once on the deck of his lead vessel, the captain looked back at the burning vessel of the far-lands which was set ablaze by his compatriots. With a sigh of relief, he collected his pet in his broad arms and strolled towards his cabin. His favorite seaman approached grandmaster of the high seas en-route and queried "O mighty captain, my dear lord; relieving a sea prey is quite untoward of your desires, are you all well at health; is there a bad omen you besiege, my lord". The captain looking blatantly towards the glittering noon sea uttered: "I know my friend and acknowledge your concern; but the man, his eyes shone of greatness to come; I don't want to be remembered but feared throughout the lands and he seemed to be the kind to make our escapades popular". "Aye Aye captain, whatever you command conforms my life, my lord" obliged the seaman and left the captain to ponder deep on his actions.

The captain looked at his pet and muttered "I do not know, why I did what I did; but for a moment, I feel, I did justice to my soul my friend". The great hiero-falcon nodded his head twice and flew high towards the bright blue sky and slowly away for his journey shall never cease. He knew there was more happiness in store for his master to behold this season.

--XXXXXXXXXXXXXXX--

3. The Criminal

"You know my dear what is a crime and who is a criminal......HaHaHaHaHa (ironic laughter brewing) they are the most precious thing in this world, they perform greatness towards the future of security. You looked quizzed, a crime is but done to make the world aware of the mistakes and unhappiness. Insecurity is vital for people to protect themselves and others. So is our friend the criminal, a master of strategy born to think and make necessary amends, you see......."

To abhor thee is a crime, but to abhor the abhorred is also one! A meticulously conniving smile delicately appeared across the infamously unknown, yet the ever talked about the master of crime, the criminal. In his external atonement and insipid satisfaction of looking into the world through his humble opening; the door; his thoughts poured out trickle by trickle.

The center of the marketplace it was, the room of doom, referred in thoughts by thee, the great criminal, was he? Hustle bustle and some somber tussle to make ends meet; by Jove, valuables, grains and goods disappeared often, but no smell no signs of the lost. The sight was serene in harmony, during the light of the day when the market place was ablaze with petty merchants, farmers and king's men; because the noise made theft and robbery smoother than silk and faster than lightning.

Born was thee, parents unknown. Lying naked in an open basket, right in the center of the marketplace. Ignored by all petty merchants, who barely had resources for themselves rather for the newborn. An old woman selling spices finally took note and acknowledged his existence. She brought him home, bathe and fed him. A dingy room for stockpiles, meant to be his home for long. By the time he was ten years old, the old woman perished without much notice or hassle. His daily bread was at stake all of a sudden. Spices were a luxury, often bought by nobleman only. But once the "mad king" commenced his tenure of the throne, spices never made a dime.

Usurped was his stepmother's business, he was left to ponder on his days ahead. He saw an opportunity out of childish vengeance and intricate curiosity in stealing bread and potatoes to deal with hunger. Soon he was feeding himself a pompous meal out of his daily exploits of his neighbor; the bald grocer. A hole in the wall, covertly camouflaged by rags and sacks to conceal his thievery. The bald grocer was rather interested in his gains than petty losses which were unnoticeable. The criminal used to take a very minimal portion to make up for his daily meal and his theft was wisely concealed in piles of potatoes and grains. By the time he was of teenage, his needs and desires expanded their horizons too. Soon the hole became bigger and the bounty larger.

He started working for his neighbor as a store attendant. His access to the stockpile became legit, so did his fat ingenious intuition for further gains. He soon started laundering grains and stocked them in his humble abode and once the bald grocer retired for the day, the criminal started operating his small emergency supplies unit for weary seamen and other petty farmers who could not make it to the marketplace in time for the day. He kept his tiny unit open at night to quickly get rewarded for his days catch at a discounted price to keep his stockpile invisible from the marketplace regulars and his pockets full of seamen gold along with other collaterals from the downtrodden farmers.

He made his profits at two ends, one from his daily wages of gains from his employer and rest from his post-market closure enterprise. But bloody greed and cunning lust for more gains and glory overcame him when he retired for the night. The starry skies, visible through the cracks of his makeshift roof, made him dream of diamonds and sapphires. His dreams were but amalgamated fantasies of his robberies; the mountains of gold bullions, emeralds, ivory and diamond hearts.

Soon he concentrated on other modes of claiming greater gains. He saw an excellent opportunity in looting travelling gypsies and foreign merchants carrying greater items of wealth. He resigned from his daily job and focused snooping and cautiously invading gypsy caravans, foreign merchant carts; when they were busy selling their goods in the open marketplace. He grabbed silverware, gold-ware and stored coins. The merchants suspected the gypsies and soon the suspicion was vice versa. A major fight broke out between the two parties involved and the mad king's guards had to intervene to disperse the public and stop the melee. Further investigations confirmed that it was neither parties to blame and this also marred the end of the great criminals thieving endeavors. It was a cautionary move to stay away from vicious guard dogs manning the unmanned caravans which the gypsies deployed in the light of the day.

The conniving lord of deceit and frivolous thievery had to move on. Soon he had another indigenous idea to continue his historic profession. He accumulated a few poverty-stricken, homeless but able teenagers to form an allegiance of thieves. He taught them to master the art, which he was a doctor off. His sleuths took to jobs in fellow merchants shops. Working their meticulous ways of accumulating food items and other grains. The stockpile was growing but was scattered to deceive the commons. Hidden in numerous hideouts and sold after the market closed.

The criminal named this evening affair, the "robbers market". The friend of the folks, the messiah of the poor and needy he became. Goods and grains sold at a discount in exchange for collaterals and interesting items which could be sold on during the day. The nightly economy flourished; more folks joined the gang under the criminal's command. Business was prosperous; the commissions were hefty. But after years of prosperity the robbing noblemen of the mad king's court found their tax profits dwindling and reprimanded petty merchants for answers. Poor farmers were questioned on lower supplies and merchants flogged for answers.

After rounds of coarse investigations a few fingers were raised on something unheard of in the commoner's world "the robbers market". The criminal was observing the proceedings of the day along with his heard of sleuths, safely secured in their impenetrable and rather invisible hideout. With swift caution and immaculate plan for action, he ordered his men to shut all night operations; putting an end to the legend of the "robbers market".

The lord of the dusk, the pied piper of all thieves, the messiah of the poor was in deep thoughts. Calculating and speculating was he for a viable mode of future operations for continuity of his elite group's wealth management. He held covert meetings of the unit to discuss possible operative ideas which could turn out to be profitable in short notice. But the guards of the crown made any day activity impossible.

One fine day, the criminal came up with the most meticulous of all plans. He ordered for a meeting in a safer hideout by the shores of the high seas. Furious he was by the order of the law; hence he declared that all his henchmen should now focus on usurping wealth from the crown. Eagerly he glared "my dear conniving bastards, the time has come to claim our righteous gold from the "bacchanal king". Booming in confidence he stated, "I rephrase, it is time to earn our deserved pride, wealth and dignity, which has been stolen by the mad king". His furious sleuths echoed his thoughts, "Yes Master, your vision is our life". Satisfied with the response the criminal further added, "we shall slowly drain out wealth from the anchored ships, by the shore of the kingdom; why wait for glory to change to doom", suggested the criminal. He was referring to all sea stricken exploits which saw the lights of the land but were drained into the royal treasury.

With an air of purpose the criminal boomed "Let's board one of the anchored ships at dusk when the seamen had gone ashore for a bottle of their favorite dry rum and cheap thrills provided by the village brothel". That was where petty farmer's wives paraded to catch an ugly eye for bloody old. With utmost unanimity the congregation of crooks thundered "so be it, thy cunning master, your order is our command". The master criminal declared the fateful date for the occasion and commanded his party to disperse.

Broad daylight fought to penetrate the dingy corridors of the hideout, the "echelon of dusk", where the criminal now resorted to. But the light never saw much appreciation, as if it was not allowed to a face to face meeting with the connoisseur of stealth; the great criminal. He had a wry smile in his face, almost believing his fate about his future endeavor.

Soon came the day, the kingdom of doom unaware, whence the stealth party commandeered by the mighty lord of evasion and stealth, invaded the only anchored ship onshore. It was a Sunday night, not a seaman aboard. The village brothel booming with the laughter of the lucky and the rage of the unfortunate. The congregation of thieves led by their master jumped on board to claim their wealth.

The ship had been freshly anchored, on Saturday night, not ample time to unload the exploits down and away to the royal treasury. The criminal thundered with magnanimous laughter upon a glance of the sea men's chest of the bounty of the high seas for the season. "Ha Ha Ha Ha, we have made a fortune my lads, keep half for me and share the other half equally amongst yourselves", lambasted the criminal. With obedient acknowledgement his henchmen retorted, "Thank you thee, thy noble master; you have made us rich beyond imagination".

The criminal wisely ordered his men to carry out the loot to his favorite hideout. The order which was immaculately followed without a second spared. Once back in the dusk engulfed hideout, a tiny lamp was lit to help the henchmen segregate the loot and claim what they deserved. Finally a strong gale blew the concealed windows and salt-filled winds burst through the window sills. "The sea acknowledges our triumph lads, see that", the criminal stated with reference to the wind. "Now disperse and keep healthy, wait for my signal for the next assignment", riveted the grandmaster of robbery.

Once his men had left, he let the tight yet old drapes of his current abode open to let the sea breeze engulf his thriving lungs. In solace he muttered to himself, looking towards the sea "Oye, my lord of the high seas, thank you for today and apologies for my deeds". With sudden sadness he let out, "If was not born to such poverty and doomed kingdom, I know not who I would have been". With an air of aesthetic confidence he glared, "But thank you thee, for recognizing my might against the bloody tyrant and supporting the lost cause, since all this is for survival, my lord".

With these words laid upfront he sulked into a sack of dried fish and dozed into his dreamy wilderness of stealth.

---XXXXXXXXXXXXXXX---

4. The King

"A ruler is but the face of God, which the citizens respect, believe and expect in glorious harmony. Of course, seeking better governance and excellent futures. The solemn voice added on and the man clad in white listened eagerly. But you see, a lot many leaders mistake themselves to be good kings, enforcement is not a friendly word. Also a just governance and long-sighted strategic moves are but colossal for building an umbrella of trust. It's the people who make a ruler, a leader unto a great king, it's their feeling and theirs only. The good king is just a hard worker. Yet the King which rules over the entire mass of land along with the seas and the atmosphere altogether far and beyond; well that king is but an equivalent of god."

Waking up early is for commoners, getting up late is for the royalty. But getting up on the meaty bosoms of his favorite whore left the king with a wry smile on his wine strained face. With an air of lust and sprinkle of romance, the law of the land uttered, "it is rather divine to wake up on top of your heavenly bosoms my love, but your king has important matters to attend and a dozen fresh bosoms to taste before the day is over". With a wholesome wet kiss on the feisty bosoms of his majestic escort, thee dismissed her. After a minor struggle to get out of the fluffy rolls of fur on the bed linen, the mad king stood on his feet by the bed and looked at his humongous royal mirror to inspect his nudity.

Looking down upon his slack features on the colossal royal mirror, the ruler of the slovenly land smirked. His wry smile broke into a peal of thunderous laughter and soon he added, "Oh my lord, I wonder if with great power comes great responsibility; of gaining weight". Patting his round flabby belly the king smirked. "Don't I look dashing, my lord", precariously added his majesty, with a trail of laughter to spice his thoughts.

His royal smirk added grace to his worldly body. Fiddling his genitals, he moved in front of the mirror and broke into a song, "Long live the king Taralala La". His meandering booze ridden belly bounced about like a wagon in a village road. A mighty lump of flesh with a glittering crown he was, the pompous fool of the land of doom. "What shall we do today, I wonder; devour some imported caviar loaded salmon or add spice to my chivalry and pop some young cherries from the farmlands", added the king with utmost elation.

The ruler of the near lands glanced left to the eternity of the grand view, outward of the iron clad window frames of his royal chamber. The bright sky has its rays bestowed upon the ultimate symbol of his existence, the royal treasury. The treasury was in a brocade of glitter which was evident through the window. The mad king smiled in divine satisfaction, and slowly turned his head to continue to adore his earthly existence in front of the mirror.

His royal servant, his beloved and most trusted aide strolled in and opened the mighty window sills to let the soothing westerly breeze revel in the royal abode. In his absolute melancholy was he, with a delicate movement of hands, he disposed of his servant. Now looking outwards, he fell into a sudden moment of gloom. His majesty muttered," What should happen If I were to be anyone else but the king; would I suffer, would I be hanged?" Looking back towards the mirror, he saw gazed at himself with the majestic crown and gleamed, "Thou shall not bother, or let thy brains play any games in my imagination, about poverty and suffering, I the great king, the ruler of this great kingdom; shall enjoy this day with divine precedence & pompous royalties which are on offer". With these words he clapped aloud to signal his royal attendants to prepare for his bath.

Strolling down to his palatial bathing chamber, he met one of his ministers waiting near the bathing pool. The minister of trade, a fat pompous man, was he; like many other noblemen in the king's court who enjoyed the crown's appointment to the fullest. He had hefty wages, designated to him by the crown, but made copious amounts of gains from bribery and extortion of petty merchants. Of course without the knowledge of the "bacchanal king"; who was always in his parallel universe of stupor and lavish extravagance provided by his fake ministers! They who continually kept him unaware of the royal loot and giving him a false impression that the kingdom was blessed to have a great king like him, who had made the kingdom prosper beyond any belief and imagination.

"My lord, when shall you sign the decree for double taxation to be levied on foreign merchants and gypsies this moon year", we need the royal treasury to have its own stature of being a noble symbol of hope and prosperity", exclaimed the rather conniving nobleman. "What do you mean, my good man?", queried the dumb king. "Oh my dear lord, you don't see those bloody gypsies and foreign merchants from far lands making more gold each day; soon will cometh a day when the treasury will bear mere chicken change for the likes of the populace", reverberated the cunning nobleman. "Ah these merchants have such intentions to my noble deeds, I was the one who granted them shelter and awarded them a life in my kingdom; and now they try to usurp thee," lamented the bacchanal king.

"I am truly honored by your immaculate vision, my lord; if you grace this royal decree, with royal insignia, I shall promise thee, the collection of his majesty's deserved wealth shall begin at once and the kingdom shall continue to prosper for more moon years to come", procrastinated the thrifty lord of trade and undoubtedly the lord of treachery. And with those words he presented the king, the treacherous scroll, tragedy of double taxation to all citizens splashed all over it". The king stamped his authority without a flicker of doub and dismissed his nobleman without reading a word of the doomed scroll.

With a few grandeurs stride his majesty plunged into his royal bathing pool, which was quite well pampered by anthuriums and poppies. Soon all his favorite set of whores swarmed in beside him caressing him with flirtish strokes, helping him pour in a glass full of ale freshly brewed in the royal brewery. In divine love and gratification, the mad king boomed in astute melancholy, lazing around.

Slow muse of the palatial harp of the royal orchestra engulfed the royal abode; manned by the court's musicians. His dreams spoke aloud, thy lips opened. "On such a fantabulous day, I would like to waive all taxes for next two moon years for all native citizens and denizens of the near lands", glared the lord of the hopeless, unaware of his earlier deeds. His whores languished in a union. Some thwarted in merry crying out loud "Yes your Majesty, we shall relay the same to the minister of finance, your personal favorite the grandmaster of the treasury. With a bent movement of the head a squawky whore signaled another mistress to fulfill his majesty's desire.

Without a moment's flicker, rushing came the master of treachery and deceit. The kingmaker, the infidel, the collector, the multiple names of the "god of deceit and bad news", the minister of finance. Glittering eyes had he, sparkling with treachery. With a grave gravity of high treason, the minister forwarded the royal scroll, the royal decree along with the royal stamp. The scroll contained words crafted with trickery and doom, stating all denizens to one half of their property and one half of their daily wages or similar worth in grains to the royal ministry of finance.

The minister stated with utmost sincerity, "My Liege, kindly stamp your divine authority on the royal decree and make your wish, to waive taxes official by law". The king without wasting a flicker of the eye, entrusting his conniving aide, stamped the cruel document of horror and smiled then glared. "May thy kingdom enjoy along with me". His majesty's cunning minister of finance vanished swiftly after receiving the order of enabling hell in the kingdom of the near lands. He was full of smiles when he parted, as so was the foolish king. Unaware was he of all the wrongdoings on his behest.

The king embracing one of his favorite whore muttered, "My love, inform the prime minister and the courtesans to be ready, I would like to attend the proceedings of my noble and just courtroom today. Obliged the whore and swiftly delivered the message to the royal guard. The king drank the fine ale with one gulp and arouse to embrace another whore was already drying him, preparing him for the fake and mere drama of proceedings in his court.

Soon a group of his fine slaves and whores dressed him in fine silk robe and emeralds crafted boots and ready was he, the lord and master; to go and attend the royal proceedings. He strode with pride towards the royal courtroom, basking in his own delusional glory. A few steps away in the paramount of stair leading to the royal charade, the prime minister smirked thinking, "Look at that moron, fat human, the one who paves my way into glory, look at him, just look at that fool". He glared out loud, once his majesty was in proximity of a genuine listener, "Oh my dear lord of the near lands, the just and infamous ruler of the kingdom, welcome to the day's affairs, how art thee".

The king replied with a pompous smile and waved a hand in acknowledgement. The prime minister led the pathway and then onto the stairs. The royal guard opened the mammoth doors of the heavenly courtroom of the kingdom of doom. Marvelous was it, the grandeur of the view and the shiny structure of the entirety of the courtroom of the cauldron of doom. The royal scribe entered, as the king approached his throne, flanked by his conniving prime minister. "All rise, the emperor of the near lands, the ruler of the mighty lands, the owner of the high seas, the protector of our people, has arrived" declared the royal herald.

The bald high priest carrying the crown laden with jewels and diamonds slowly staggered towards the throne. The king wore the emperor's robe, with minimal help from the royal mistress. The priest eventually strode up the stairs up to the throne and crowned the mad king, after blabbering a fake prayer. Finally shouts of "Hail thy lord, long live the mammoth king", engulfed the courtroom. The mad king finally occupied the mighty throne carved out of flint and decorated with fine gold and emeralds to give the royal chair, the authority and grace it deserves.

Addressing the dignified crowd gathered in the courtroom, the noblemen, the jesters, his favorite entertainers from exotic lands, the travelling foreign merchants, his favorite courtesans and escorts", the king glared. "My fellow noblemen and women; may your lives prosper in this beautiful land, may your lives be pompous and filled till the brim with merry and joy". The attendees retorted, "Hail", thy pious king, justice and love shall prevail in our lands as long as you live; my lord".

With a wide smirk appearing momentarily in his broad face, due to the praise; the king continued, " My dearest prime minister, let us begin with the legal affairs of the day and then you can introduce me to the guests of my court for today, who have travelled from far lands for my divine accordance". The witty yet cunning prime minister humbly retorted, "My lord, you have given this land more than enough already today by authorizing the new taxation law, there are no pending legal matters for the day, I am afraid my lord; especially in the lands of such a just king like you". Continuing he added, "Your land is now officially the happiest lands in the entirety of mother earth My Liege".

Further continuing his speech laden with motive, the prime minister stated, "I propose my lord, to introduce the foreign noblemen present today and post which we can celebrate this pompous moment with fresh wine and dazzle of the exotic gypsy dancers of the far-lands, who have graced us with their presence in your court today". The king nodded in acknowledgement and waved his hands to start the proposed proceedings.

The prime minister signaled the royal maids to serve the wine and commanded the foreign merchants to present the king with the intricate royalties, valuables and rare artifacts they were carrying. One by one they bowed before the mad king and gifted him with rare emeralds, sapphires and invaluable art. Wine poured in each glass, held by humans in royal attire. The king boomed with pleasure when his glass was filled with exotic rose wine. He raised his glass, cheering to the royal crowd. The courtesans glared in amalgamated enthusiasm, "Thank you my lord".

The exotic dancers jumped and thumped in the central vicinity of the courtroom. The royal orchestra booming in union supported the dancer's moves with immaculate precision. The royal escorts flocked near the king, who was busy pouring wine in the bosoms of one of his finest whores and vigorously licking it off with enormous pleasure. A few ministers exchanged glances and one of them blabbered, "look at that old fool, he is busy with his own stupidity, totally devoid of our exploits; Oh I love this fool so much". Laughter followed along with the continued entertainment delivered by the royal escorts and exotic dancers.

At the end of the evening, the king was in a drunken stupor. Unable to even stand up on his own feet. A few royal whores helped him up and dragged him back to his royal chamber. Once in, he suddenly gained the confidence to walk and soon dismissed the royal brigade of escorts. Slowly staggering towards the royal mirror, he undressed himself. Soon was he, naked like a newborn urchin, but still wore the crown to mark his authoritative presence.

He was still smiling and analyzing his bulky figure when an eerie voice spoke to him in utter urgency. "You ignoramus clown, you pathetic sodden bastard of the highest kind,; look at you", glared the voice. The mad king was startled and comprehensively surprised at the sudden intervention and invasion of his royal privy. He looked around in sudden anxiety to locate the source of the grave voice, like a disturbed monkey in a jungle. The king commanded, "Who goes there, who is the infidel who dares to speak to the master of the near lands, in such vile demeanor, produce yourself before thee".

After a short while later the disturbed king looked back at the mirror in utter horror to find a crimson-colored version of himself with a crown standing right next to him in it. Laughter filled the royal chamber, the king started to sweat since there was none next to him in reality, only in the mirror there were two versions of him". He threw a wine glass at the mirror and the royal mirror cracked in two, but still firmly stood thanks to the mastery of the carpenter. Now there was a clear division in the mirror between him and his mysterious adversary.

The red imaginary version of him stopped laughing and added, "You horrendous, fat fagged monkey, you inglorious little imbecile, wake up when it's early, do you know at the least, who you are and what you are meant to do"? With complete vengeance, he continued, "You are the son of the old just king, the new ruler of the mighty throne but yet you have killed him again in his deathbed; again in his heavenly mortal state you and your nonsensical deeds along with your murderous greed continue to murder him. "You are blind to prosperity and the existence of your own people, your frivolous deeds have brought shame upon this land and now you are left naked without any authority and respect", stated the unreal adversary.

The king glared in disbelief, "Oh shut up you mischievous and unkind being, I have done no such thing as you declare, I am the great ruler of the near lands, which is in harmonious prosperity as we speak". The king's imaginary adversary gleaming in an ironic smirk replied, "My young baboon, who looks old, I am a part of you, I am not allowed by the law of nature to lie to myself, please understand this fact my foolish living body; I beg you, kindly get hold of yourself and your surroundings before it's too late". Saying these words his majesty's imaginative yet real form disappeared into thin air, leaving his highness in complete delirium.

The ruler of the kingdom of doom, the scum king sank into his bed and stared out of the royal window in delusion, into the grave darkness outside.

---------------------------------------XXXXXXXXXXXXXX---

5. The Union

"Sometimes you meet certain people due to pure fate. At times it's accidental, but you see it's written. Everybody has to meet somebody, who might be anybody in the beginning, but the entire episode turns out to be a magical experience, where time stops and busy Mother Nature halts to check what just happened! That's how the gods created the concept of friendship, a camaraderie beyond the understanding of nature, an absolution of surreal bonding where individuals bask in its shadows for greatness or not, but are all happy in its journey."

Still was the sharp blue waters of the high seas, yet stirred were the minds of the two humans in the floating gondola. Even the Sun god had bestowed all light rays of astute attention on the two merchants from far lands, floating on the tiny gondola; cast in the sea. The mighty high sea gale had momentarily disposed of his identity on the very day and transformed into a silent whisper of a breeze; in order to keep tabs on the evolving argument between the two lone survivors at high sea.

Arguments are but fragments of uncertainty in an unstable mind. So was the brief episode of incongruous behavior portrayed by the two tired merchants in the gondola. "You thieving bastard, you traitor; you who sold our land our beautiful far lands; just for your mere life and a few words of that crooked captain from the near lands", exclaimed one merchant to the other who had talked to the captain for the commiserations of their wellbeing.

The other merchant glared "You fool, you shall never see the pious thoughts and justice of the great man, who let us cherish all senses today; you fail to understand the meaning of long life and a great human's kind nature and goodwill. The conniving loyal far land merchant retorted with sudden elation "Ha ha ha ha ha ha ha, how long will your treacherous praise last; look there is one of our finest ships from far lands, revenge now is inevitable". The other merchant tried to put up a futile argument but the cunning far land loyalist pushed him overboard onto the arms of the high sea, and started rowing mercilessly towards freedom and revenge; towards the mighty far land ship.

As the gentle yet brave merchant was falling into the arms of the mighty high sea, a piece of log fell along from the gondola; prompting a divine intervention on his survival. He swiftly swam and got hold of the lifesaving yet a nonliving piece of log to float along. A few seagulls hovered around in utter amusement, in an otherwise uneventful few days in their recent lives.

-------   --------   --------   --------

        --------   --------

In a flurry of swift strokes of his ever industrious yet criminal set of hands, the criminal cracked open a huge padlock in his hideout. A wry smile broke upon his dubious face and his pride shone. With his ever-increasing confidence he muttered "He He, finally the old fools chastity belt of fortune is broken; the master of absolute disaster takes it all".

Earlier in the day he had commanded one of his finest sleuths to grab hold of a similar padlock; resembling the lock of the royal treasury. The master of stealth had his ever penetrating eyes on the largest storage and epitome of the symbol of wealth; the king's treasury. "This mid-afternoon of glorious importance of gratification, I behold to myself; Thy shall conquer what is rightly his", proclaimed the grandmaster of thievery. Without a moment of haste or sparing a heartbeat the sole proprietor of wisdom and governance in the art of conspiracy stood. He knew what was in store in the astute plethora of dreams and endeavors which he had ever dreamt off; that the very act of looting the treasury was of absolute importance, also the ultimate goal of his life as a human and for the sustenance of natural law and order of this very land.

The connoisseur of loot strolled in absolute harmony, through the narrow streets lining the shore, feeling the sun god's grace and gentle stealthy breeze of the high-seas, on his covert journey. His destination was set, his goal secure and expectations met. From the thick foliage of vegetation he could see the back door of the embodiment of wealth and palpable prosperity of the human existence of the state.

Suddenly the skies went dark and the clouds barked; in the symphony the rain god's poured in the tears of joy. The criminal smiled and brought upon his hood, slowly progressing towards the heavenly gift of stockpiles of gold. Soon he reached the shadows of the mammoth structure; right in front of the backdoor to the glorious and ever talked about the royal treasury of the kingdom of doom.

He struck a match to light a candle.

Sturdy was the pole and still was the mast, of the swift far lands ship. Strong was its bow, huge was its size; with ease it carried a hundred seamen all armed to the teeth. The intentions were clear, the master of the ship had met the merchant; the cunning survivor. Revenge was set by the order of the far lands navy and the entire fleet of twenty ships now rowed mercilessly through the high seas with clear precision and a zeal to conquer the mighty captain's exploits. Moreover to put an end to the beast of the high seas, and also to the ever-emerging tales of the great captain's might and glory of his infamous high sea excursions.

The dream was turning into a nightmare and the mighty captain was not happy with what was on display in his deep slumber; shaking and shifting profusely from one end to the other in his grand bed at his cabin. Similar was the scene that broke outside in the deck. A smiling seaman talking to another suddenly felt a piercing pain in his chest and looked down to observe for the last of his breath, the tip of an arrow which had penetrated through, from the back of his body. Soon more arrows followed and them they rained in harder than the pouring natural tears of the rain god's. One seaman fell after the other. The captain's favorite seaman looked around in horror; the entire near lands historically renowned fleet were burning and slowly sinking into the arms of the high seas. Only the captain's ship stood tall, but more men were mowed down by the incoming swarm of arrows.

Running came the captain, to acknowledge the loss and his defeat; snatching a cutlass he slashed and beheaded the first incoming far lander, who attempted to jump on board his war machine. Glaring at his favorite seaman, he exclaimed "Retreat, I order, retreat; make it flashy and swift". The seaman quickly gathered a couple of half injured hands on deck and maneuvered the ship; back towards the near lands port with extreme urgency and incredible swiftness.

The far-lands fighters gave a prominent chase, but their experience in rough weather situations at sea was rather evident when the only ship; the captains one, vanished into the layers of darkness and fog at high sea. All other ships of the mighty captain had fallen; most loot lost at sea, some nabbed the fighters with help of the far sea merchant, who had spat on the captain's gesture of goodwill.

The angry weather god's thundered when the captain scanned the shoreline of the near lands. Sad was he, the great connoisseur at the fallen gold, destruction of his beloved ships and his best seamen lost at sea. His favorite seaman sat in a corner of the main deck, near the mast and sobbed. The hiero-falcon descended out of the dark sky and sat on a piece of log in the deck, near the sulking captain. The captain laden with sorrow as well with anger thwarted "Why have you come now my friend, when all is lost; have you gone blind". The great bird, the eyes of the high seas; bowed his head in absolute grief and shame. He knew that greed had kept him ashore near the far lands, where he was feeding on easy prey.

One of the seamen dropped anchors when the ship was few notches off the shore. The dejected and heart fallen master for the high seas jumped out of his ship into the shallow waters of the shore. He started walking, looking up at times towards the rain god's; as if to seek answers for such fallacy which was unknown before this very moment. His favorite bird flew and sat on his right shoulder, acknowledging and praying so that no such mishaps occur to his master for infinite moon years to come.

Convoluted and morally polluted thoughts revolved in the head of the dejected grandmaster of the sea. His thoughts blabbered in his head "the thieving mad king and his conniving ministers will murder me for this; them undeserving bastards won't accept any mistakes which puts a hard stop to their gluttonous habits". Now muttering with agitation, nearing the narrow road leading to the backdoor of the royal treasury, by the side of the royal chamber, he glared "I shall murder that bastard king if he doesn't reason with me today; I shall not talk to his thieving ministers, I shall confront him directly at his chambers". With ever-growing anger and astute determination he strode on boldly towards the royal chambers, now passing by the backdrop of the treasury. Suddenly he saw a source of tiny light, a lit candle come to life in the shadows behind the royal epitome of wealth and he slightly changed his course to inspect its agenda.

———— ——— ———— ————

———— ——— ——

Ignorant rains poured on; on an ignorant land laden with ignorant commoners and also on the ever ignorant ruler the messiah of doom, but yet he slept on. The ruler of the near lands was devoid of the knowledge or existence of the affairs of the day; post his fore night engagement with his own colored imaginary version; his secret but real adversary. The swift rain and the sudden angry gale of the westerly wind commanded his royal window to open and it did. Heavy teardrops of the ever-important god of rains, projected angrily at the "bacchanal king" to try and wake him up to the solemn reality of his fallen state.

The determined droplets of the anger of the weather gods landing incessantly on his sleeping majesty's face. The drowsy ruler of the near lands made an enormous effort and finally opened his eyes to reality. He inspected the mild darkness growing outside his window and the rain pouring in. He stood and went to close the window sills to avoid the anger of the rain god's, stumbling towards it just like a newborn; all naked except a crown on his head.

Suddenly a small bright light appeared behind the royal treasury.

The ludicrous king ignored it thinking it must be one of his royal guards performing his duties with due diligence. He was about closing the sills when he froze with utter horror and shock. His mysterious adversary; his own imaginary yet real version, was standing, smiling and waving at him a few meters from the window; out in the royal gardens. The red imaginary version of him was waving at him to come with him and also with one hand was pointing at the source of light behind the treasury.

The playful red imagination of the king was jumping around towards the light and at the same time calling upon his real self with flesh and blood to join him in his short expedition. The mad king smiled and sat outwards from the window to jump. The imaginary red version now smiled and started running towards the source of light behind the royal treasury. The king jumped out and started running over the poppies in his royal garden; trying to follow his soul. After a mild sprint halfway through he realized that he had lost sight of his mischievous adversary. His majesty blabbered "That fool must have joined the one with the light". He continued his brisk sprint towards the small light behind the royal treasure; now completely soaked in rain.

He soon reached the backdoor of his treasury but in utter dismay observed that there were two other humans present there; one hooded individual holding a candle and the other a worn seaman who had a falcon on his right shoulder. There were no signs of the mysterious adversary. The criminal acknowledged the sudden change in noise behind him and turned; he saw a naked man with a crown and a seaman with a fierce-looking bird on his shoulder.

Without a moment's haste and in complete surprise and irony of the situation, the captain burst out laughing at the very sight; he was pointing at the naked clown with the crown. The criminal joined in too, in absolute harmony; laughing and pointing at the king. Knowing that no other alternative or art of deception, in such a tight situation could change his current destiny. The king observed the two for a while then started laughing and pointing at the two souls in front.

There was a brief pause in the laughter of all three. But the pause was momentary. Soon all three souls continued to laugh at the top of their vocal capacity and the rain poured in and the thunder grew louder. To add to this insane orchestra, the hiero-falcon started hooting aloud too.

---------------------------------------XXXXXXXXXXXXXXX---

6. The Discovery of Irony

"Laughter is the best medicine", the statement itself is an understatement when the three most prolific characters of the godforsaken land had initiated it. Louder than thunder it was, the conjugated laughter, only the mutual understanding of the meaning for the same was aloof. Soon the weather gods were baffled by this unexpected and sudden change in the muse and retreated its blessings of thunder, lightning and rain, in total confusion created by the three messiahs.

Finally tiredness prompted the three to cease their extended melodrama of unintentional irony. Huffing and puffing for a breath of fresh air, the captain uttered, " Oh my God, been waiting for such laughter since days, I had forgotten such luxury in recent days, thanks to you my naked lord, what an immaculate clown you are". The king frowned at such a vile gesture and declared, "How dare you call me a clown, look at you, one with a bird on, you who seem to look like a jester of the high seas".

The captain's confidence took a divine dive for a new low with those words from the ruler and he muttered, "You may be right to call me so and here I was all pumped up to talk to the vile king, the blind one, but look at me, the one who has been mocked at sea".

The mad king retorted, "I am not blind you imbecile, mind your tongue you high sea scum, you shall forfeit everything if you continue to address me, the great ruler of the near lands in such inappropriate manner". With humongous laughter and to respond to the proclaimed master of the near lands the mighty captain lambasted, " Ha Ha Ha Ha Ha Ha Ha, my apologies dear clown, I fail to acknowledge your astounding acting of the highest pedigree, pardon me, my little master, I propose, since I have lost the purpose of visiting the king now at this very moment, since its futile and a complete waste of our time, yours and mine, I plead you two to join me in my humble abode and share a few drinks and of course some freshly smoked fish too".

The stealthy yet silent spectator finally stated with utmost precision, "I pray you two seem to be a perfect match for the night, it's quite ironic this sudden melodrama of comedy but all said, thank you both for such silly and unwarranted yet enthralling entertainment". The king probed with growing curiosity, "Insipid comedy eh, let's forget for a moment this unthawed irony and discuss your presence with a lit candle behind my safe house of fortune at this hour and in such dangerous weather, shall we".

The captain intervened with a spool of patience and cried out loud, "Oh come on, you two join me I beg, I need good humor, some good food and definitely some perfect form of liquor to see a formidable end to such a horrid day in my life". The conniving master of crime, smelling an excellent opportunity for a perfect escape from the probing situation and of course to re-plan his return for his deemed high stake of fortune at a later time declared in a compassionate tone with further comprehension, "I agree and accept the noble seaman's proposal for wine, dine and probably divine comedy, come on my dear majesty, I request your grandeurs presence in such an important affair right at the heart of the near lands".

Both the master of thievery and the lord of the high seas burst out laughing at the sarcasm blown proposal to the mad king, unaware of the monstrous reality of the situation. The bacchanal king graced their laughter with a wry smile and then thee stated, "I generously do not mingle with commoners but I am also tired of the luxury of my royal chambers, the lord of the near lands agrees to your kind yet bourgeois proposal for a change of weather of course".

The captain momentarily stopped laughing and added, "Let's go now then". Without a moment to spare the mad king glared, "Alright then, I the ruler of this very beautiful land, command you to guide the way to your courteous dwelling, your majesty the king shall grace it and make your livelihood for the day". The king and the criminal let out a volley of laughter, yet to maintain the continuity of the royal episode of events, jumped in to act. The captain appeared to play the role of a royal scout, bearing an invisible flag of near lands authority and the criminal marched like a royal bodyguard behind the naked king with a crown.

Naked was he, not only body but soul as well. His emptiness was marred by astute corruption within his own royal walls. But now his new expedition paved the beginning of a fortuitous yet eternal route to enlightenment, the road to sacred knowledge, the understanding of the state of the population and their grim existence". The legendary trio traversed through the heart of the near lands, with an air of utmost confidence. The most distinct but unknown in reality yet infamous lords of the near lands strolled through the streets without a stare of doubt or even a mere raised eyebrow.

Aloof were they and so was the population in terms of the current reality of their worldly existence. If only the gods would point them out glaring from the heavens on their stoic yet paramount omnipresence. The damp yet evident chaos of extravagant poverty and unhappiness was dearly palpable in the stark surroundings which the three infamous musketeers of the great near lands were treading trough. Petty farmers scavenging through garbage to find fodder for the night. Hungry men and women roaming around the marketplace, begging for a meal, equivocally the poor shop owners shooing them away. Semi-naked skinny damsel's drinking water out of the sewers by the roadside to quench their burning thirst.

Observing the state of affairs of the doomed kingdom, the king was aghast and beyond belief, gazing around the mammoth mess of his own creation, with extreme abomination glaring in his eyes. His eyes couldn't believe and his brains stopped functioning, thy heart cried out loud. Now he could see his mysterious adversary dancing around the middle of the road, smiling and pointing at the mayhem with short bursts of self-choreographed steps to present the magnanimous mess to his worldly self, as if to say, "Now you see the pain and suffering of your lands, the real kingdom of doom". Tears of self-inflicted acrimony and nihilism poured in an uninterrupted manner. Strolling was he in his own lands, barren was it and with an equally empty pocket of gloom trotting along.

On the rare contrary of the panorama of this legendary situation, the captain was in a divine muse, as if he had found solace in this amalgamated chaos, a self-structured enigma governed and directed by celestial pleasure, in the company of his newly found yet majestic congregation. The criminal on the other hand was keeping his pace in an equated digression to the master of the high seas and also in turn making sure he is in the middle of the slow-moving brood of legends. Confirming the fact that his identity is well concealed with the hood on and definitely making sure to check on his safe distance from the unusual clown king, in turn hoping the clown was providing him appropriate cover from behind. He was content yet cautious of his stage, an immaculate actor of treachery was he, the master criminal, but in the present a mere seeker of unknown camaraderie and friendly companionship, ones who did not judge his intention's or his past history of larcenous activity.

The infamous seafarer, the meticulous light-fingered human and the comic king trotted towards the old seaman's humble abode, which was quite abundantly visible now. It was a log house just by the near lands old navy pier, on the right side of the fish market. One could smell salted fish all day long from a distance. The hiero-falcon now understanding the captain's light muse amongst his new companions, felt he could let his master enjoy his day and also the prospect of feeding on fish, his only possibility on fulfilling his day's meal and conquer his hunger made him fly away towards the thick fish smell.

Now slowly the mini troupe hovered by the fish market when the mighty captain noticed a familiar mariners face and glared out loud, " Oye, grab three fine red herrings for me my lad, will ye". It was none other than his favorite seaman, sitting was he, depression engulfed, but once he heard his master's voice, a little smile protruded and stayed on, his owner had arrived and so was there a hope of continuity. A raised hand acknowledged the progression, one towards hope and a future filled with great days at the high seas. With the smile still lingering over his tired face, the favorite seafarer moved to fulfill his captain's commandment.

In a few moments, the trio had arrived in front of an old ye bold passage made of the finest mahogany, one which had a rustic anchor for a door handle. The indomitable captain smiled and turned to welcome his unusual companions into his sacred abode. But his smile disappeared as he saw the tears of the clown king. With intrigue and compassion for his fellow guests of honor, the captain queried, " Oh my lord, what makes my good nobleman cry, who dares to upset my king, cheer up my friend, no tears of sorrow allowed behind this ingress.

The colluded master of crime looked back startled to find the comic yet royal human in a sad state and the master of deception went into a melodrama of emotions himself. The prime robber of the near lands stammered, " Oh my dear friend, one who is pure to this earth and is naked to confirm the same, why is thee so sad, is it our company which thy despise, kindly cheer up.

The master seafarer commanded, "Come on lad, sadness is a disease, spread throughout these lands, people embrace it with honor, yet without knowing its reality, do we need it at this hour". He continued, "Me, you and our curiously hooded friend over here, we need to retire for the day and share our experiences and sorrows,

I beg you, please don't be selfish in hiding or burying your secrets today, since I am an open book man, learning my ways and traits on the go".

The naked monarch replied with a sudden burst of confidence, "I love both of you, as you are, for giving me the prime pleasure of experiencing such a day, to evolve as a human, who was unknown of the current and real perils of his own society and its soiled wellbeing. The captain let out a burst of thunderous laughter and declared, "I agree my dear friend and honestly your act is one of the most premium kind, please allow me to render my hospitality for the day on your behalf, I request you both to enjoy my humble bearings for the day without a thought of despair or malice".

With these words the most experienced czar of the high seas pushed open the gateway to his ample yet magnificent dwelling, this particular action also marked the ingress of the trinity into a stratosphere of natural understanding, one which was, without doubt, the best stages of their ever-evolving lives. The inbred messiah of the high seas squandered through the rich doors of his magnanimous cabin, his current and eminent companions followed him with a renewed excitement of forbearing adventure set for the future.

Exquisite was the interiors, décor of stolen silk and gold of the far lands, carpets of rich linen and fur, windows facing the treacherous yet majestic high seas, waves dancing in front as a muse for the legends to embrace. Furniture made of the finest teak wood and cutlery of stolen silver. Old ship wheels forming household paraphernalia and rare rubies and emeralds the finishing of his utensils and of course armory in the display. Large swords and cutlasses which had slain a thousand able seamen, shields of ivory and steel the protector of many, before their final breath, adored the sharp blue walls of the disputed ruler of the high seas.

The criminal's mouth was now wide open in shock and utter disbelief, due to the magnanimity of the collection, one which he didn't possess and also of the piety of the captain's invitation of such goodwill, which was unknown to him, altogether he was spellbound into oblivion.

The ruler of the near lands was still in mourning, one which he had never observed. The captain lead the way to his personal chamber and then finally pushed open the door to his balcony, which was rather a mini pier, leading out to the sea. A fine piece of wood of the deodars formed the dining table laid out in the personalized pier of the high seas seafarer. He looked back and waved at his guests to join him in the magnificent view of the high seas.

Lukewarm sea breeze added to the pleasant brood of the situation. The mighty captain took a seat, soon followed by the others and the seagulls honored them with their chirp. Without a second to spare the captain's favorite seaman brought out the finest brew of the land and poured it onto three glasses set for the legends. The captain stood to make a toast and glared out happily, "It is evident and clear that it's us three who rule these lands without doubt and fear, even the seagulls, water and elements of Mother Nature are acknowledging the same, look at them, the birds hovering around in honor of the congregation.

The overjoyed seafarer, the captain's first hand burst out through the doors with finely cooked red herrings and served a portion each to the legends of the near lands. The criminal now in absolute melancholy blabbered, "Thank you Oh great captain, this is the first instance, where one has shared food with me without malice in their hearts or an obligation presumed". The captain thundered in satisfaction, "Oh my dear hooded friend, life is but short and obligations too many, happiness is rare, I wish to share it when felt".

The master of the high seas then turned towards the sobbing ruler and stated, "My dear friend, does our company still make you sad, is there anything we can do to cheer a clown, one who usually keeps everyone in muse with his mastery in comedy". The mighty ruler of the near lands wiped his tears and declared, "Oh my dear seafarer, I love you and our hooded friend for letting me see my country, my own lands at its nascent stage for the first time in my life with my very eyes. I have always believed thugs in my high court and imbeciles who fill me with wrath and treacherous details of misfortune as well as misinformation. I knew not that my kingdom was in such an abysmal state and my fellow men and women torn off from relishing basic amenities of human life".

There was a serene silence which followed, even the seagulls glided near without much noise, without even flapping them wings, the waves became sober and the water still. The king further added, "Thank you both for today, I have started to enjoy your company, hope this learning continues". With these words the ultimate rule of the near lands flipped open his glittering crown and let it rest at the table. A funny thought bore in his mind and he stated, "Oh and by this act, the emperor of the great near lands is fully naked now, along with body, mind and soul".

Both he and the captain burst out laughing, but the criminal was completely busy investigating the originality of the crown. His eyes shone wide and his face grew grave. He picked the crown and examined it at length like a great sculptor or a seasoned jeweler and glared, "This crown, is not an ordinary prop you use for any acts, this is truly the crown of the emperor". Looking at the king he queried, "Are you saying, you are the King, my Lord?"

Abrupt silence intervened the laughter of the king and he acknowledged, "Yes my dear friend, I am the king of these lands, apologies for my neglect for not wearing any proper clothing, I had woken up from a deep slumber, please pardon my habits, I should definitely make amends to it as well as improving the living state of these lands going ahead, I promise you that, my good lad". With the greatest of concentration, the master of the high seas examined the crown and retorted, "I cannot believe this divine yet royal comedy of errors, I thought you to be a clown king, moreover you real image prior to this which I had in mind was of an arrogant ruler, one who didn't understand or care about his fellowmen, but this is not completely true as you have proved you do care".

 Continuing his speech he added, "You, my lord have realized today the true state of affairs with a clear heart, which was necessary and I was present to speak to you on behalf of my recent tragedies at sea".

With these words the captain went glum and his mood filled with elation disappeared. The great king thwarted, "My good god, tell me you are the mighty captain of the high seas, the ever feared messiah of the waters, you who my ministers always claim to have fulfilled the necessities of the lands, yet they lie about the fortunes lying in my treasury, as I know now, they must have devoured every last penny of your hard work and passion at the high seas".

The mighty captain retorted with great endurance and pleasure, "You, my lord have spoken of the deserved truth and you are and will be my beloved king, no barriers can defeat my purpose of serving you, I shall always be your humble servant and kindly pardon my sins of the recent, I have failed you gravely sire and this heavenly mass of land by my deeds at sea, but I promise you My Liege, good days shall come and them shall stay within us forever".

The curious criminal of the near lands finally declared, "This is but royally rhetoric, I who is the biggest thief in these lands, know more of these lands and their longevity more than you both". A smile full of passion and pleasure appeared on his face and the masterful criminal uttered the truth for the first time, "Having said all of this, I will also declare that I have been a very small man with a great vision for stealth and robbery so far, my final heist was to devour the riches in the royal treasury of yours my lord, but yours and the mighty captain's divine intervention has changed my intentions and moreover the future of my cause". The criminal further continued, as the other two legends were now in utter shock and held gaping open mouths to demonstrate their unbelieving state of mind, "Yet with utmost shame and sympathy for such noble souls of the highest kind, I would like to dispense of my activities and devote my skills and livelihood for the betterment and the progression of this great empire on earth".

The ruler of the near lands retorted with renewed pleasure and utmost satisfaction, "The significance of the failure to lead a great community, the likes of this land has made me think about its prosperity and I promise you livelihood shall prosper hereon, but you, my friend the greatest robber, the criminal I have heard off during palatial accords in my high court, accusations against you are unjust, cause you had a reason behind it, it was for making your blind ruler see clarity again and I totally agree on your vision for a better and prosperous near lands".

The mighty captain now thundered with utmost euphoria, "I the captain on the near lands mighty naval fleet, promise greater might and conquest at the high seas and beyond, I suggest war with the far lands hereon, I shall strike and give my blood and flesh to see these lands bloom again, My lord, Oh mighty king, order the next phase of action, your majesty".

The king boomed with surety and astute assurance, "I hereby declare war on the far-lands, let it be at sea as well on land, I also waive all taxes of these lands and I shall see to it myself with my own eyes to the prosperity of every fellowman, woman and child, moreover I want this legendary feast to continue, but my dear captain, kindly provide me a robe, my nudity is getting unpleasant and it's definitely getting colder over here".

All three legends of the near lands let out a peal of thunderous laughter. The favorite seafarer and the personal attendant to the captain ran in with a fine silk robe and helped to clothe the king. The criminal poured more fine ale for all three and their glasses clanked, but this time the toast was lauded by all, "Long live thy purest near lands, long live all humans beneath the blue sky". Even the birds chirped and sang aloud to mark the beginning of a new era, a period of war and peace combined.

---XXXXXXXXXXXXXXX--

7. The Exploration of the Divine Truth

"Truth, nasty word you know. How we see it, or hearing about it is fine. Humans always mistake by questioning it. It is simple, "Truth" is what it is, and it's real. And the unreal is a lie. The druid turned angel smiled and blabbered on ...."

A rather bizarre episode in the kingdom of doom had rewritten its ideology and history for good. One which was eternally unique and exceptional in nature. The sun gods had retired for the night and the moon king was cherishing the regalia of company below and that of the starry skies. Beneath this space odyssey, lay the three fabled trios, on the personal pier of the captain, they joked, they laughed out loud into the sky, they strategized, they mobilized their futures mentally. They laid on their backs looking straight at the starry skies and glared at the moon god, who acknowledged and approved the communion of such mythical nature.

With an iconic gesture of uncharted glory, the undisputed ruler of the near lands glared, "My dear beloved captain and my purest little criminal of the highest kind, I request you, my lovely legends to bless my soul and be a part of the forbearing journey of mine and yours combined. I politely demand your presence in my royal chamber, the royal courtroom and of all royal affairs going ahead.

Bearing an imperative pause to the continuity of the amusement, the great captain stated, "My good friend and my great lord of these lands, I shall accept thy command under one condition only". The captain, in the most inclusive of manner, added, " I want me and the great connoisseur of stealth, to be a part of a rich gypsy party, from the far lands, who are visiting the royal ministry, trying to pay homage to the great lord, that is you My Liege and you accept us as your guests, let us in for the commencement of the utmost critical passage, into the entirety of the royal escapade, and of course all this to happen naturally without raising an eyebrow, even the both of us will be dressed appropriately for the cause".

"Just so that there is no suspicion or concern about us in their minds, I mean your thrifty ministers my lord, all in all, a perfect stage play to sow the right seeds of progression herewith", exclaimed the mighty captain. The now, visionary king concurred, " Seeds of gold you mean, the epitome of succeeding actions to come, a bright thought, this shall pave the way for the rightful entrée to the royal affairs and the beginning of our immaculate yet influential vigilante of the proceedings of the state, in a legitimate manner of course".

The notorious observer, the great criminal added intricately, "After which my stealth and espionage skills will come of fruitful usage for the progressive communion, I believe, I will be of much decisive help then, My Liege, as I want to repay all my misdeeds in a mutually beneficial purpose going ahead". Both the captain and the king let out a humongous smile to grace their iconic faces and nodded in appreciation and communal acceptance of the significant verse which shall uproot all evil from the calamitous state of affairs of the kingdom for years to come.

The captain stated with divine harmony, "Oh my God, the moon god, the one governing us and the stars, my dearest majesty, I lie you not, this man over here might have committed petty crimes or even greater, but his heart is of the purest kind and the brain incomparably the best in the far and near lands combined, including that of the high seas, I concur".

The king with a sudden heavenly burst of energy stood, acclimated and glared, " I have a brilliant idea, once we are done with settling with all paramount operations of the state, pardon my excitement, let us go on a sea excursion and a necessary conquest of the far lands henceforth, as you had earlier desired, O mighty captain, moreover the presence of our friend, the infamous criminal makes our seafaring expedition a rich and righteous affair in terms of mastery in strategy, at the magnanimous waters in between both lands, I pray, please lend out a thought on this regard my dear lads".

The two notable and the closest friend of the ruler of the near lands nodded in an astounding union on the future course of action. The mighty ruler further added, "Our unity and undoubtedly trust in one another is an armament more fierce, a weapon just and governing all the fortification and unity of these lands and that of the sea's, right under the eyes of the moon god".

"With unconditional melancholy and confidence of wisdom be piled on, a tyrannical yoke my destiny had become, until I met you noble yet extraordinary souls, now this rocky promontory which has become of our lives shall cease to exist, may this holy fellowship mark an end to this torrid affair in the history of these sacred lands and that of the high seas". With eyes gleaming like a set of meteors, the conscientious fire of affirmation and attainment of the ultimate truth, along with a heavenly sense of purpose the ever intelligent criminal declared, "You were meant to have the life of a king my lord, Oh supreme ruler, your longsighted vision for guts and glory shall make us indestructible at sea and in the hallowed lands all together".

Out of the stark darkness of the nightly sky, the old friend and pet of the solemn captain swooped in and landed on the dining table; it let out three prodigious yet heart-rendering squeaks of honor and modest respect of gratitude for the continuity of good reasoning of the three legendary humans. Free were they, the legends of legends, a perfect escape from retribution from the unjust and the undeserving. Soon the colossal bird, graced the right shoulder of the captain to mark the beginning of the voices to unearth the vocal vacuum of natural desire, realization had evolved.

The captain patted his most cherished friend of the high seas and in honor of it stated, " My dear friends, this over here is my eyes of the high seas, this is no ordinary bird, but is the original governor of the seas, it knows every tide, the very space of blue between us and the far lands". The hiero-falcon understood his master's purest thoughts and bleated in noble recognition and his devotion to the cause ahead, which he accessed from the unusual yet angelic conclave.

" Enchanting bonding of the absolute quality and tremendous vision, I believe your revered companion's competence to the fullest my dear Kaiser of the seas, this incredible bird is and will be our

protector when we traverse across to conquer the far lands,"
declared the king. "Oh my god, we have everything we need, let us
pounce upon the glory which awaits us with open arms, let us
embrace greatness and change the course of the winds of fortune
towards thy deserved lands", exclaimed the master of stealth.

The amicable banter, the loud chatter, prodigious laughter prevailed
until the moon god retired along with his starry friends and finally
the three glorious musketeers fell on their backs on the pier and fell
into an eternal repose. One which was filled with the sweetest of
dreams, and nature around obeyed the serene notion for calmness,
still was the sea, the breeze polite and the seagull's lull.

The sun warmed the three legends in the morning, the wind
whispered in their ears to be cognizant and to address the affairs of
the prized kingdom. The king was the first to embrace the light of
the day. He shrugged off his slumber and rubbed his eyes to grace it
upon the magnificent view of the high seas, adored by the waves of
the high tide and the hovering seagulls dancing in the humming
wind. He smiled and put in a noble effort to wake his dearest of
comrades.

Soon all three were up on their feet. A bright thought shone in the
king's mind and he commanded, " My good lads, let's make haste
while the sun gods shine, I pray, we get to the royal court at once,
but before that my dear criminal, tell me, my lord, is there a
possibility that you can get apt costumes for this pompous royal
spectacle, one to dress this mighty sea captain as a rich far lands
merchant and you, I believe a royal messenger, to make

exceptionally credible characters to behold for today's royal proceedings".

With complete acknowledgement and frivolous laughter the conniving master of deceit glared, "Yes Sire, your majesty, what an innovative thought, I already see the seeds of truth sown in the heart of the grandeurs of these lands, I pray Sire, I shall take my seafarer friend at once to my hideout to prepare for this historically decisive day, I have volumes of such attire waiting to adorn and to grace such episodes of glory".

The king nodded in appreciation and the captain added in total corroboration, "I am all yours my resourceful little friend". On a pompous note the king pronounced, "In the time being, I shall sneak into my royal chambers unnoticed and command my ludicrous ministers to announce a caucus for today's royal proceedings at my high court". "Do be there in an hours' time at the royal gates, I shall make sure the guards receive and welcome you with honor", with these words the mighty ruler of the near lands picked his crown, hid it under his robe and waved a quick goodbye to his new assortment of friends and hustled to get back to his chambers in order to set the plan in action.

The other two legends obeyed the course of action and ran stealthily, led by the criminal towards a very intricately secured hideout at the far south of the kingdom. The birds swooped in low in a notion of their attendance to a critically extraordinary manifestation in the history of the lands. Trotting rapidly through the road less taken, just by the beach facing the seas, the legendary duo could now see an abandoned lighthouse. The master of larceny looked back and smiled at the captain, who smiled back in ratification. They had arrived, at one of the most uncanny of the master criminal's hideaway.

Soon a secret adversary, an able henchman opened the doors in utter confusion to see an unknown entity accompanying his master. The criminal made a signal with his hands to mark the fact that they were among friends and so did the abettor, now a smirk bearing his rugged face. The legends now enter the dark interior of the grandmaster of crimes secret refuge, soon they reached a room, rather an abandoned cabin, which was filled up to the brim with far lands exploits, robes, furs, footwear, jewelry and armory of the highest kind.

The mighty captain's jaws dropped in unmitigated amusement and awe of the knowledge of such a stockpile existing in these very lands. He patted the criminal's shoulders and stammered, 'My God, umm... you have some copious amount of loot here my friend, I hope we would find the right attires and accessories here before the hour is over". Letting out a brief laugh of compassion, the criminal stated, "Do not worry my friend, I have already seen what would be apt for a rich merchant, which you are going to enact".

With a swift movement of hands he waved his aide, a partner in crime to come over. At once he came and the criminal whispered in his ears, the items required for this immaculate feat in the history of noble deceit. His favorite hands ran to fulfill his master's orders. Soon he returned with a glittering robe of fine silk, embroidered with precious jewels to elevate its existence and the sword of a nobleman. The criminal nodded towards the captain to try them and so he did. In a whiff of his magic wand, he had turned the captain into a merchant, without an aroma of doubt.

He dispatched his mate to get felicitous footwear and jewelry to complete the divisive dressing of the master of the high seas. Soon with the help of the notorious sleuth of the near lands, the captain had transformed comprehensively into a merchant of the far lands. He walked towards the mirror in the cabin to do a final scrutiny and was astonished beyond belief. "Who is this? My dear friend, I do not recognize him, is it me? My good God, by thunder you are an artiste more than a thief my lad", stated the captain in recognition of the abilities of the grandmaster, the criminal.

"Ha ha ha ha, this is the easier part of your act my friend, difficult is the purity of soul, your character has to enact, hope you will come out victorious in the latter as well, just follow certain elements of your character and say which is necessary, you shall triumph in the realistic of plays which are about to begin at the heart of these majestic lands", said the criminal.

Without a moment to spare, the special fugitive ran back with the maestro of crimes attires and accessories. Worn were those without a blink of a human eye and ready was the duo for the royal challenge in the near future. The criminal smirked at the captain and so did the captain in return as if they were two young school kids who knew nothing rather than spreading mischief amongst neighbors with an air of continuity for more such episodes to transpire.

Two fine robust camels were ready when they approached the egress of the abandoned lighthouse. They rode with purpose and incredible zeal towards the heart of the near lands, on towards the royal gates, towards kick-starting a profusion of heavenly tales to commence.

The majestic ruler of the near lands had reached his royal window without getting noticed but getting in was rather the difficult part of the affair. His flabby belly was making it extremely difficult to sleep in through the sills and with great eternal energy he finally struggled and fell in his chamber with a large thud. Rushing came to his royal aid, his favorite servant to help his majesty and stated, "My Lord, your Highness, is everything fine?" the king was in a hurry to make sure the plan of action was absolutely flawless. With urgency he blared, "You fool, can't you see your majesty on the floor, help me up and immediately fetch for my prime minister". With apology in his eyes and soul the royal servant added, "Pardon my sins my liege". And with these words, he thy servant with a gladiatorial effort helped the fat king upon his plump feet.

Soon he rushed out to fetch the conniving prime minister. The king in the time being rushed and changed his clothing without seeking his royal concubine's efforts in dressing him, especially since time was of the essence. In a flash he wore his finest robe, made of exquisite linen and silk, turquoise in color. He flipped on a heavy set of jewelry, gilded with gold and a few intricate pieces of rich emeralds, sapphires and of course rare diamonds. He picked his crown and wore it. And finally he grabbed his old yet magnificent royal symbol of authority, the finest sword of the near lands, which has been a silent spectator for very long, but not anymore.

With a wry smile the king picked up his sword and carried it along, on his way outside his chamber. He could now see his thieving prime minister walking with a brisk pace towards him, with an air of intrigue as to what this sudden meeting was all about. Uneasy was he, since generally, it was he who knew how to manipulate the situation and extract exactly what he wished for, but this time he had a sense of divine urgency, just unknown was the cause.

The king cherished the look on his highest ministers face and he glared at him, " Prime minister, hustle when you can, there are a plethora of engagements pending for the day, I want purpose and zeal when the sun god still shines his blessings for the day, come on now then, make it quick". The minister finally reached within earshot of the majesty huffing and puffing for air and bearing a quizzed look on his face.

Finally, he queried his master, "Your majesty, you had called upon me for some important matter, for your royal affairs, I pray, what is that thee wants today, a fine bottle of port wine or shall it be an assortment of the finest deer meat we have from the latest expedition recently completed by our finest hunters of the lands, give your command my lord, I shall see to it being fulfilled at once".

The king snapped at him, " You moron, immediately gather all royal courtesans and ministers, an entire lot of royal fools in the fortress of our high court, I need to start the most prolific proceedings of the day, and sure there is fine food and wine for later, some for the esteemed guests attending our court today". The prime minister was taken aback by such vile gesture and unattainable task thrown at him and stated, "My liege, is everything all right, we have no dignitaries attending for the day or any royal affair to tend to". The king with further anger added, "everything won't be fine anymore, especially for you, if you wish to spend a moment more questioning my command, leave immediately and make certain of the gathering in a flash, you need to know nothing further, you are dismissed".

Bewildered was he, the thieving prime minister, but was bound by the duty of the crown and the kings governing vocals to run in a flash to set things in order. The king now swiftly trotted behind the royal courtroom and then made swift way towards the majestic palatial gates where the royal guards stood. He commanded one of his imperial guards to step forward with a wave of a hand. The guard was in utter shock to confront his majesty and immediately stood in front of him in astute attention. The king leaned towards him, whispered a few words to him and left.

The guard now focused his attention outside the royal gates with utmost sincerity at the task assigned to him by his visionary ruler. The king meanwhile rushed back to the courtyard and found the members of his royal orchestra lazing around and graced them with a profound vengeance, " You bloody mongrels, what did the state hire you for, to sleep around my palace?! Is it, start playing your finest tunes at once and may that last until the night falls and the moon gods go to sleep, get to it immediately without failure, or I shall behead you and feed your rotten flesh to the hawks for fun."

Them they feared such exclusively spoken words, a few cello players pissed their pants, but all assembled together and played the finest ensemble of musical glory the land had ever heard. The mighty ruler had an uncanny wry smile on now and a heart in peace, yet his mind made him hustle towards the palatial stairs, heading towards the royal courtroom. In a few leaps of faith he was in its heavenly doors and with a wave of the hand he ushered his courtroom guards to open it and he entered.

Attendance was abundantly up to the brim, all courtesans, royals and thrifty ministers had gathered, the conniving ministers had even brought in a few, fake merchants, imposters trying to pass by as far lands merchants. The kings smiled at such stupendous stupidity and with minimal efforts took his seat of the throne.

A raised hand of the mighty ruler made the plethora of attendees to stand in honor and the royal orchestra to pause for a brief moment. The king uttered with utmost confidence and divine purpose of the wellbeing of the nation, "my dear attendees of the royal court, many a priest, governors and warlords have attended my heavenly court's proceedings, but today mark my words, is of the most special kind, in this day I expect an infamous far land merchant and an unequivocally important noble messenger of their lands.

With further direction and epic motive for greatness in mind he continued, "I expect a humongous welcome for them and special honor bestowed upon them, and honor which was not realized before in this very court, may the gods be with us today to embrace this truly great moment along with us humble souls, I command my royal guardians, my dear priest to assist our esteemed guests into the courtroom and make sure the proceedings begin once they have adequately been addressed."

The priest was in shock yet hastily ran towards the exit to see to his master's words getting fulfilled. Soon he returned with two other humans, who were with absolution, bearing the description of the legendary king. Smiling were they, all three of them, when their eyes met and finally destiny beckoned. The king rose and bowed for the first time in his life in front of these finest humans of his own lands, the captain and the criminal. Extremely well-disguised were they.

The mighty ruler raised his hands to mark the start of the proceedings when the criminal stood by his seat near the cunning prime minister and the captain next to the lord of utmost thievery, the minister of treasury. The entire courtroom boomed with the following words, "long live the great merchant, long live the royal messenger, long live our just king." The imposter of the highest kind, the prime minister with vile motive to undermine these proceedings declared, "Welcome you two noble beings to our mighty king's high court, a place for just causes." But his words were slashed in half by the divine intervention of the master of con, the notorious yet stealthy criminal.

He snapped, "Thank you dear prime minister for such kind words. My dear Majesty, you certainly have the finest men representing you at the magnificent courtroom on your behalf, your honor, I the sacred far lords messenger behold before you the royal impediment of our loyal court and the finest merchant of our lands to greet you on your behalf; kindly accept our gratitude and blessed be thy, for years to come.

The criminal took a bow and directed a quick flirtatious wink at the majesty for his acknowledgement of his enthralling act. The king without the notice of his royal attendance returned a wink in appreciation and waved a hand towards the captain for introductions. The captain took a bow, one to behold, a most royal in nature and graced by a precarious mind, added in glory, "your highness, I the far land's richest merchant bring you the finest emeralds, pearls and armory of gilded gold and of course the finest and smoothest silk of the far lands, to grace thee and his dominion for your association today, I pray thee, may this humble beginning of our esteemed friendship be a permanent one."

The captain took another bow and an impeccable yet unnoticed wink to concur with his consideration of the plan of action, which was strategized by the trio on the previous night. In came the royal guards carrying the far land's loot, which the criminal had ordered his henchmen to maneuver in order to speak for their presence in the royal court. The king quickly inspected them with gratitude and directed his guards to cache it in the royal treasury, with a wave of his hands.

Without letting any of his majesty's pompous yet thieving ministers to utter a single word of deceit, the master criminal glared, "My lord I hope our humble yet hearty gifts, filled with immense goodwill, provide your majesty with the satisfaction of our deemed gratitude, moreover I and my fellow men have some intricate matter to discuss for the betterment of the two kingdoms, I request My liege to grant us the opportunity for the same, that would be all from my end Sire."

With these words he took a bow and endorsed the king handle the rest of the interesting journey of discovery, wisdom and destiny of the near lands. With angelic yet covert intentions the criminal, let the king to initiate and direct this promising future on behalf of the trio. The king stood and glared, "Thank you, both noble souls of the far lands for such gracious gifts and kind words, words of passion and forbearing of harmony of the two lands, I hereby order my prime minister and his fellow ministers to organize a grandiose feast, a royal luncheon followed by an imperial dinner in our heavenly dining hall."

Continuing he added, " We shall, my dear noble messenger, definitely discuss our future course of actions in regards to the wellbeing of our lands in private quarters once the feast is over, I, command my ministers to act upon my words at once to the royal order, the court dismissed". The prime minister was left in complete desolate of belief at what had happened yet with the fear of unforeseen consequences, promptly gathering his spool of thugs, the ministers, to prepare for a royal luncheon.

The royal orchestra glared with union to honor the occasion. The king stepped down from his throne hugged his two legendary friends and escorted them out of the courtroom of doom to the royal courtyard where three magnanimous thrones had been set. The royal chef on the other hand ordered his finest cooks to start preparing the finest of feast for the day. Soon the courtyard was filled with royal courtesans and dancers of far and near lands, professing their artiste, with the finest of moves, the best of wines poured throughout and then the three-spoke one by one in an undertone.

The captain nodded at the king and the criminal, and stated, "I believe the grains of fortune have been sown right at the heart of near lands, with a royal decree of course". The king let a wry smile out and declared, " Your acting has been of the finest kind, so was that of yours my dear friend, the great criminal, your strategy for the exploration of the divine truth of the affairs of my royal court has taken a favorable shape."

Raising his glass towards the king and the captain, the grandmaster of crime uttered, " thank you, your majesty and my dear captain, I love you both for such an opportunity but time is of the essence and a lot of unavoidable tasks pertaining to the stronghold of this holy communion still remains, I shall start my act of stealth and imminent collection of invaluable intelligence at once, I shall go ahead and blend with your colluding ministers to gather more baroque knowledge and stolen gold from the treasury, I pray, I ask your leave for a short while to spy amongst your noblemen to investigate their state of affairs. Kindly allow me to do the same, My Liege".

The king nodded, the captain smiled and clapped towards the dancers and the criminal disappeared only to appear again amongst the core group of ministers, discussing women, wine and snuffle for the truth. The royal orchestra played the tune of victory, a victory never known before, one pf primal importance, one which hummed with purpose for the winds of change which had engulfed the kingdom for good.

--XXXXXXXXXXXXXXX--

8. The Moment Of Truth

"The uncertainty of victory and defeat keeps reality thriving for the glory of the "tomorrow" and yet tomorrow never dies. The petty humans follow this prophecy without thinking that it was but a rule created by the creator for them to live and to prosper."

Scavenging for a piece of fine meat was the conniving prime minister. Hankering was he, avarice brimming in his nerves for meat and more, but the quintessential master of frugality, the ever so illustrious master of crime, the infamous criminal, intervened at the ultimate moment to put a blunt stop to his desires and in the process pushing open a new door, one which lead to the discovery of the buried truth.

The truth the kingdom of doom deserved to know, one which can edge the kingdom closer to the enlightenment of the possibility of goodness and greatness for ages to come. The criminal intervened, "My god, dear prime minister, you pry for a piece of fine meat just like you salvage taxes of the state". The prime minister let out a cunning smile and retorted, "You have some keen eye my dear friend from the far lands, meat is sweet and so are the taxes, all waiting to be devoured by the law". With a wry smile and an air of delicate touché, the criminal added, "Fair enough, my lord, taxes I bet must be well governed by you in these magnificent lands, I presume".

The fraudulent prime minister added , in a lower note," You see, we have but just recently levied double taxation, if you have any influential message which you say you carry and if thy feel I should know of it in advance, maybe there is a likelihood you shall benefit some royalty too, before you sally". The criminal sensing a chance to further investigate and gain headway into the larcenous affairs of the murderous prime minister, intricately added," I agree my noble lord, what is a friend for, if not with benefits, I shall inform you of the news I bear, the moment I get a chance, in private of course, far away from this madding crowd". He blinked an eye and continued," But just to be sure my prize lays safe, I wanted to have a check, I pray the great prime minister, tell me, is the exploits of the double taxation well shielded, is it concealed well amongst these fortified walls and can be hauled without raising an eyebrow".

The nefarious prime minister smirked patted the criminal on his right shoulder and whispered, "You worry too much my dear friend, the premium cache, collected from taxation has been stored safely, with astute vigilance provided by two of my favorite royal guards in the royal granary behind the kitchen, it's easily movable through the back doors of the palace and payouts happen regularly for royals and of course to gift vital friends like that of yourself, noble envoy".

The criminal gave a warm hug to the pilfering prime minister, one to mark his fake acknowledgement to pacify the high treason and stated, "We are of like minds my governor, I am looking forward to accomplishing primal business with you". With these intricately equivocal yet decisive words the criminal let out a grandeurs bow and took his leave to regroup with the King, unnoticed of course.

The mighty captain on the other hand had befriended the minister of treasury and both were seen visibly enjoying each other's company. The captain gleamed in his achievement and pried to know more about the tragic affairs of the state. With an air of utmos calmness and a tone piercing his prey, he added," My good minister of the treasury, you, my lord have compassed volumes for the kingdom, and of course I bet, a lot for your fat pompous belly, I presume, I pray you to continue your admirable act of service to all, also if I may Kindly do keep humble far lands merchants, the likes of mine conclusive, in your noble thoughts".

The minister of the treasury was in a drunken stupor, yet he stated in extreme satisfaction, without knowing the captain's intentions, "My friend of the far-lands, the treasury is but just a symbol, I have hidden gold well-stocked in the near lands garrison, just off the royal navy piers". With a muffled laugh he added, "There is a famous yet eternally foolish captain of the near lands, whose exploits in the high seas are well known; he submits his exploits every time he is land-borne, once he is done at sea, I tell you friend, all of the gold and the glitter is stored in my secret hideout by the navy piers, without that seafaring moron's knowledge".

The captain was filled with the sheer rage of a very unique kind, but to salvage the possibilities of the future he avoided sabotaging the situation and bowed in an epitome of a fake melodramatic posture. The venal minister continued, " I shall most certainly share some of my exploits, if you provide me with invaluable information of the far lands trade and merchandise, also their schedule of maneuvering the same at the high seas and trading ventures to near lands my dear friend".

The captain let out a sardonic smile in acknowledgement and stated, " My lord, I shall and will always be your most trusted compatriot in commerce between them lands and that of the high seas, I promise thy, that when the time is right and definitely when we are alone, out of eyesight and that of the prying ears, I will relay all that is deemed paramount for such an honorable and yet powerful soul like you, my master, at this juncture I let thee enjoy the exotic booze, meat and women at the disposal". With those intelligent words, the captain bowed and took his leave. He then swiftly disappeared, sniffing for more significant intelligence, to fortify his desires and that of his two legendary friends.

The king, the symbol of eternal confidence of the kingdom, was savoring the frivolous acts of his legendary friends, keeping a keen eye at their astonishing progress and subtle incursions of tremendous importance. He was in but divine muse, one brimming with astonishing satisfaction and vision for future prominence. He commanded his royal chefs to bring in more exquisite meat and cherished drinks to honor such a gratifying moment. The gypsy dancers reveled the moment with their gracious movements. The royal orchestra was playing at its utmost best that day, a pitch brimming with perfection and chivalry of the highest kind.

The master seafarer with electric pace and measured steps leading herewith unto the greatness of the near lands approached the ever disillusioned and timid minister of internal affairs and homeland security. He greeted the minister with a warm hug and a pat on his back. The minister had a diabolical expression worn on his face. The captain guided him to his senses with charitable yet shrewd words of wisdom and vision, "My dear commander of the near lands, the eyes and courage of you who lead these vast lands is but understated, you have my lord , made sure the near lands continue to breathe and prosper with your immaculate vision and proximate governance of course.

The interior minister, one who never was commended in such a high note of ovation by anyone in his lifetime, struggled to believe his ears, yet conveyed his affiliation towards the divine truth in plain language, one which all poor souls relished, for their prosperity and longevity in these treacherous lands. With a gulp of fresh air he added, "My noble lord of the far lands, I honor your presence and I also acknowledge such a divine gesture. I have never been treated with such elegant words for my royal forbearing or granted the dignity of my command."

With a huge heave of genuine gratitude, he added, "But since you mention my presence with such grandeur, let me warn you, my Lord, the decisions of the state or of its safety is not one of my deemed tasks, unfortunately, the prime minister has made all of this his with the consolidated acknowledgment of the consortium of slanderous ministers and foot soldiers under his command; I am just a petty flag bearer of shame'.

The captain was taken aback with such humility of the nascent truth, yet with a steadfast manner of righteous enforcement, he added, " It is extraordinarily cordial of you to describe your situation of a pittance, but time is of the essence and your position of reality to look back at the foregone days of humiliation and wasted glory, I pray for my friend, kindly let me know of the even-handed and faithful men at your disposal for the elementary actions to foresee today's matters of the utmost importance in terms of governance and ruling of this great empire below the moon god's presence".

The general and governor of security of the near lands embraced the mighty captain dearly and stated," I apologize, my lord, O great captain I have known you and your deeds of sacred responsibility to the kingdom, even when we were worn out but utter madness driven by the greed of the prime minister and of his multitude of voracious ministers, at a moment I was convinced that the legendary ruler, our king was involved in the plot; I was paid puny bribes to stay clean of any affairs of the state, definitely of any undertaking related to security and safety of my fellow men, but you, my lord I cherish, so does all poor and downtrodden yet pious souls who constitute this kingdom".

With ingenious vigor of enthralling confidence, he further added, "We know you as the messiah of the high seas and that of these lands, one who fights for the symbol of peace and unanimity, which we ministers forgetfully declare of, you are our freedom and as of today's statement of the declaration by our visionary king, I am assured that the right set of levers are in place for divine intervention, my lord, without any haste; kindly direct me to foresee any commandment of yours, because I know whatever you say I shall envisage and fulfill. And anything you say is the real law of thy lands and that of the high seas".

The captain beamed in honor of such a colossal gesture, the picturesque yet famous way of letting the person in the conversation know of the acceptance and clarity of mutual desire. He bowed and told the governor of security to gather his trusted forces for impending actions to discern in the coming days and then he slipped away towards his throne set beside the king in the courtyard. Only one of the three thrones were occupied so far, one where his dearest king sat on, with a warm smile gleaming on his face, just to portray his majesty's satisfaction at his noble friend's achievements for the day.

Soon the captain reached his throne and sat on it with a hand laid on the king's arms, he finally patted in confirmation and affirmation of the ultimate knowledge of the truth and beyond. The royal orchestra now played a somber tune, laughter and frolic filled the vibrant muse of the royal courtyard. The criminal had finally slipped away from his position amongst the royal swindlers, the ministers of course. He appeared next to the king and sat on the throne designated for him. The trio was in eternal bliss.

They were satisfied with the keenly executed incursions in the realm to unearth the ultimate truth. The captain and the criminal in turn informed the king of the matters of the state which needed immediate attention, they also exchanged strategies that commanded prominent action. The king ordered the captain to secure the prime minister's loot and bring it back to the royal treasury. He also authorized the criminal to seek aid from the captain's newly made friend, the minister of *"internal affairs"*, to seize the cherished gold and treasure which the mighty captain had secured, yet which now sits in the secret hideout of the larcenous minister of treasury.

The two legends departed in a flash to oversee the mammoth task on hand for the restoration of the divine glory of the near lands. The sun had set itself to rest and the moon god appeared, excited to know more of the proceedings below. The king thundered with the ever growing passion and essence of maximal forbearing, "I hereby command all to savor the evening at this grandiose royal gala, let the music flow free, along with thy wine, I thank you all, let there be concord in these lands for many moon years ahead.

The melody of the royal orchestra cascaded down upon each aristocratic soul present in the royal gathering. The king saw his mysterious adversary, an impression of himself in red, dancing around in the muse, in front of him in the courtyard. His adversary now smiled and took a majestic bow. The king responded with a wry smile, a smile to enforce peace and tranquility, a smile in the ratification of the divine contentment in this prevailing situation of the stately affairs.

--XXXXXXXXXXXXXXXX--

9. An Enterprising Excursion

"A journey has no meaning or existence if there is no thought of eternal cause, behind it. A cause either just or unjust, one with action or none. But the purpose of the captain's swift traversal through the royal escapade towards the back doors of the royal granary was for a just cause. A journey in which he was accompanied by two of the most loyal guards, whom the noble interior minister had left at his disposal."

That very moment the two disloyal guards were visible strolling around the door as directed by the slanderous prime minister. The governor of the high seas glared at them with supreme wrath, "Ahoy you feeble men, I command you to surrender your arms at my feet and adhere to my order to retreat, or I shall pounce upon you with terror, the terror of such magnitude and purity, one which even the gods have never observed throughout their tenure of heavenly vigil".

The two larcenous royal guards bore a diabolical expression with their heartbeat reduced to a faint whisper of the gods of death, at such humongous threat being delivered by the mighty captain. The captain drew his majestic meaty blade and flashed it in front of his troublesome opponents and they froze to death, observing the scene. The red eyes, filled with vengeance, vengeance so great even the gods would have retired for the night and so they did, the moon god retreated along with his friends the stars.

Pitch darkness governed the plethora of existence below, only the couple of flickering candles shed their doubts of light into the matter. Two swords clanked when they hit the floor, and knees bent they were, two seditious guards, scared to death on the concept of challenging the captain. One of them had the fortitude to bleak and let out a few words, "Pardon me sir, my lord, we are just mere servants of the prime minister, hired for a few shillings of gold in order to foresee our ends meet in this tyrannical kingdom, spare us our lives and we shall promise to disappear and never return".

The mighty captain let out a burst of thunderous laughter, "Ha Ha Ha Ha Ha, you petty downtrodden mongrels! scavenging for food with treacherous larceny in mind, I pity your existence, but I am no cunning soul who murders a man with no sword or no just cause of direction in mind, I order you to help me and them fellow guards behind, on our intricate task at hand to secure the royal gold and transfer it back to where it truly belongs".

With further poise and passion he glared, "The King trusted you and you took a royal vow to serve him in thick and thin, in bad weather and in good with all your might, now it is the time to prove your existence and that of your service to the kingdom, fail me not, cause if you do you shall not exist. Now stand up be men you were deemed to be and fulfill what the gods above you created you for". The two guards obeyed the captain at once and stood to follow his command.

The captain barged into the royal granary and his jaws fell at the sight which lay before him. A notable hillock of gold, sapphire and ruby lay before him in the storage meant for grains and livestock for the royal denizens. He nodded and smiled at the four guards at his disposal to commence the divine act of restoration of pride to the kingdom, the movement of the destined gains back to the royal treasury.

Pitch dark was the serenity near the royal garrison when the troupe headed by the master criminal reached its proximity. Since it was a rather unaccounted for and a rare secret hideout, only used by the pilfering minister of treasury for caching high seas gains, it was unguarded. The master criminal smiled and flipped the key out of his pocket. With minimal efforts he cracked open the old padlock which guarded the sacred gold. Now he commanded his fellow loyal guards to commence the transfer of the same, back to the treasury with a cheeky wink of an eye.

The scene was set, serenity defined, the muse melodious, breeze divine. The king took a magnanimous gulp of fine wine to quench his thirst and felt the glory of the two of his beloved legends of friends, back in a flash on their royal seats beside him. He almost cried in joy, yet he managed to let out a positive note of laughter to address them. The legends united now exchanged glances of commiserations. Finally all three let out a peal of outrageously prodigious laughter.

Victory is but for the legends to embrace and even the gods knew this victory was portended for certain glory of the kingdom. The king stood and made a grandiose speech, "My dear royals, thank you for attending such a glorious day of progression and existential harmony of this very dear kingdom. It has been a very long day, I shall not bore you any further, I hereby declare the end of this gala night and mandate your gracious presence in the royal courtroom tomorrow at high noon that would be all".

With these words of the King, the royals dispersed and the three legends, arms knitted around each other's shoulders trotted nonchalantly towards the royal chambers. The moon god and his friends beamed with pride at the three legends. The captain radiated with ever-growing contentment and sighed," Phew! What a tremendous day with the utmost primal yet cherished events unfolding at this very day, I am but extremely content at my actions and that of you two my beloved friends, tell me my lord, O thy mighty king, what is in store for the night". The criminal let out a short speech in tandem, "The night is but young and so are we, my lads, almighty king, tell me, what shall be done to mark an end to this day in a pompous note".

The king was but all smiles and as he patted his fellow legends and glared, " My dearest friends and denizens of this unique kingdom, it is you who are my most prized possessions, I suggest we bathe in the royal interior pool, drink some good wine of course and definitely strategize for the "*tomorrow*". Finally, the nature's creation, the finest trio known in the near lands strolled into the royal chambers and jumped into the magnificent pool. Soon they were flanked by exotic courtesans and royal escorts, the finesse, the beauty and then the wine poured. And it poured on for long. The captain was busy devouring some elegant, wet yet meaty bosoms of the finest royal whore.

The great criminal was in another celestial world, one fine royal courtesan had dived underwater and was she sucking hard on his thrifty cock. The majesty was adoring such frivolous behavior and himself was found busy caressing two fine gypsy femme Fatales. Laughter echoed into the night, so did the orgies which followed, a mass act of sexual desires, a million shades of grey. The humps, the oomph's, the aaahs and ohhhss' glared out into the night sky, the solo cello player and his modest artistry were lost in translation of the consolidation of the orgasmic accord that was buzzing at its divine best.

The king got tired of fucking his finest escort and let out a mere sigh. And his monstrous dick obeyed his sly command and puked out a load of royal cum into the glorious hole it was temporarily accommodating. The whore smiled when thy cock was retrieved back to its noble quarters of the king's crotch. The king kissed her forehead and dismissed her. He waved another hand at the plethora of royal escorts and they too left. The trio was alone now, they laid on their mighty backs. The criminal assertively added, "So tomorrow it is, the day we declare the crimes of the state and arrest them Machiavellian ministers at fault and of course deliver the declaration of war upon the divine far lands".

The king declared with valor, "I pray you have outlined marvelously my friend, the scope of a prodigious proportion of governance and the succeeding declaration of war of the lands which is lying far and also of the high seas, I reckon, is it not right for me to add the seas, assuming, in our war driven proposal, O my dearest captain?". The captain was in a divine symphony, relieved was he, yet war-ready. With utmost urgency he nodded, "You are correct, my lord and so is the criminal, and there shall be war, both in the lands and that in the mighty high seas. The calamity shall cease by tomorrow and good old days, the glamour and glory shall overcome and engulf our petty souls forever".

The king clapped and in came his royal servant, rushing was he. The king commanded for preparation for his bed, for the three to repose. Repose it was, the divine proposition for the rest of the night, a most gratifying act now left to the trio to achieve, and act most deserved, one which they needed to make such a heavenly day's work rest in peace, along with the entirety of the kingdom. They fell on the majestic bed and in a flash dreamland bestowed upon them with unconditional grace.

The Sun god took center stage yet the trio was in divine repose. There was a massive knock on the window panes of the royal chambers, the captain's eyes, the mighty hiero-falcon was knocking on it with his murderous beak. A most required act to awaken the wisdom of the kingdom on such an auspicious day. The king was awake and soon was the other two legends. The king smiled and trotted towards the window and let the mighty bird enter the chambers. With great satisfaction he added, " O mighty bird, the eyes of the kingdom far and wide, welcome my lord of the high seas and thank you for relieving us from our slumber to tend to this majestic day which awaits us ". The hiero-falcon hooted once, in acknowledgment of the king's gesture and quickly flew to land on his best friend's shoulders.

The captain patted his friend and gave him a few hazelnuts to devour. The criminal suggested with divine precedence, "My lord, dear majesty, time is of the essence and the hour most eminent for a grandiose royal decree, I pray thee, kindly announce for a grand attendance of all royals in the courtroom today". The king thundered with royal pride, "I agree, I shall call upon my attendant at once to see this through". With those words he clapped hard and the royal servant appeared in a flash and took a bow. The king added, "Good lad, rush out at once and relay my message to the prime minister, ask him to gather all royals at once in the courtroom". The servant obeyed with another bow and rushed to fulfill his master's royal order.

The trio got ready for the proceedings of the day and let the hiero-falcon adore the royal chambers. The legends cantered with immense pride, out in the courtyard and exchanged glances with an amalgamation of divine purpose, of the acts and speeches in hand at their disposal to fulfill on the very day. The royal attendant ran towards the king and took another majestic bow and muttered, "Your Highness, the courtroom is filled to the brim with all your royals my lord". With those words the servant took his leave and the trio walked briskly, climbing the mammoth stairs to the royal palladium of governance, with an air of majestic sovereign pride. The gigantic doors of the courtroom opened and a plethora of noise, musical and not, boomed out of it to grace the legends.

The conundrum of the royal drama of the unknown was evident. The ministers had a look of utter shock and uncertainty of the day's affairs, even the orchestra as well understood the muse and played on, in a faster more determined note. The captain and the criminal, rather the far lands merchant and the royal messenger took to their thrones next to the ministers of interior, enact well devised to let the proceedings of the day take a consolidated and unanimous predicament for the governance to sustain in the kingdom.

The king finally settled beside his throne and wore the royal crown. He raised a hand to stop the royal orchestra and the royal announcer glared for all to stand. Each and every soul was on their feet when the prime minister broke the silence of the royal stage and intervened, "My Lord...". But the king instantaneously interrupted his speech and glared out loud, "Oh shut up you thieving mongrel! You who stole from the king and that of the kingdom, its fortune, its pride, its existence, its harmony, I command the royal guards to capture this swindler of the highest kind and throw him into the royal dungeons to be beheaded at a later time, one I please, be apt for such an occasion".

The guards came up and pounced upon the prime minister and led him away to the dungeons, while all along the way he begged and prayed for mercy which eventually fell on deaf ears of a rather enlightened royal gathering. The king continued his royal yet divine prophecy for retribution of just and fair affairs of the state, "Moreover, I command you, guards, to arrest this conniving minister of treasury and make sure he is well tortured by the whiplash, not thousand but five thousand lashes for his sins of treachery and looting of our royal symbol of economic and harmony; after sundown, you shall take him and throw him in a dingy cell in the royal dungeon".

The guards tended to the king's declaration at once and imprisoned the minister and dragged him out to the royal courtyard to be whipped. Similar drama continued and the pleadings of the thieving minister were not entertained, nor anyone there to question the king's actions. The king had a wry smile on his face, whence he glanced at his legendary friends. He nodded towards the infamous criminal and took his seat at the majestic throne.

All royals took to their designated seat at the royal courtroom. The criminal stood his ground and added, "My dear majesty, almighty god, I the far lands' royal messenger bring some very sad yet important message which I received this day from one of my trained pigeons. The news is grave, the far lands have started preparations for war with the near lands, I suspected the vile king of my own lands at such acts of vandalism and treachery. I hereby declare my association with the near lands and my unconditional support to thy king, my lord, the justest king known in the lands and that of the sea".

With those words he bowed and took his seat at the high court. The king smiled and nodded towards the captain to proceed with his act of valor and strategy for the times ahead. The captain reading the royal plot for the greatness of the kingdom stood on his feet and took a majestic bow, a quite grandiose one and with morale scintillating through his body glared out loud, "O my dear lord, his majesty, as our dear messenger has stated, this saddens me and I understand his position and reverberate similar intentions, I might be a far lands merchant but I have an immaculate understanding of the high seas".

With an air of authority he further added, "I request thy majesty to declare war on the far-lands to unite the two nations and also the conquest of the high seas, for I believe the two kingdoms shall prosper under your visionary eyes and your impeccable governance". With these magnanimous words of wisdom and grace he let out another majestic bow in honor of the mighty King and took his seat. The king smiled, a very divine one indeed, filled with utmost pleasure. He knew the ball was in his court and the court was always his. He rose with ever-growing pride and declared with divine urgency, " I concur and I believe your honesty and vision, I agree on the same, I hereby declare war on the far lands and that of any vessel bound afar, from this very moment, I command both of you to prepare for such a historically paramount event at the earliest".

He took a deep breath and glared, "My dear minister of the interior, I command you to help these two noble souls at all cost and I trust, thee shall fulfill the same with honor. I want to be seaborne with both of them, with a mighty force of a fleet never seen before in the high seas; filled with able men and women who are but real patriots of this kingdom". The minister of interior and internal affairs stood, he shed a tear of joy and added with glorious pride, "My dear majesty, please forgive me for being slack and lame prior to this day, but I promise you my lord, a king so just, I shall make sure by Jove that all operational matters of garrisoning troops, fine swordsmen, the resurrection of the near lands fleet and that of its pride shall begin at once with utmost precision and redefined respect for such a divine providence".

He bowed and let the king declare for one final time. The king gleamed in pleasure and stated, " Let the preparations begin, long live thy near lands and the far lands which shall fall to us soon and of course, the almighty shall help us in this act of valor; moreover the high seas shall be ours too. Court dismissed!" The trio exchanged glances, stood and finally departed towards the doors of the courtroom. The minister of interior smiled at the trio and opened the mammoth doors. And they descended down towards the courtyard in arms of love and gratification around their heavy shoulders.

The whiplashes on the now bare red-back of the minister of treasury could be earnestly heard, the king smiled and nodded at the two legends. They nodded back and dispersed to ascertain the king's declaration of war at its utmost prime fashion of accordance with the deeds necessary to see it fulfilled. The Sun god gleamed, as the king progressed past the lashing of his tyrannical minister, on towards his royal chambers. The cello player played a slow divine yet eternally pleasing tune to mark the satisfactory progress of the most heavenly day of the history of the kingdom.

The captain broke into a brisk walk and then onto a sudden canter. He stopped at the gate where the minister of interior was awaiting his arrival atop a horse and a spare one for the legend. The captain jumped on top of his magnificent beast and out of nowhere the intelligent bird, his favorite being flew in and adored his shoulders. He smiled and patted it and finally nodded towards the minister in acknowledgement and direction for the foreseeable actions to mark the beginning of the proceedings for a seaborne expedition. One so great, so magnanimous, not even the gods have observed or besieged upon. Them they rode with the urgency of purpose into the dust created by the hooves of the horses, further towards the royal pier of the near lands, into thin air towards their objective.

The criminal on the other hand disappeared from the royal escapade and reappeared in his treasured hideout, finally, he whispered in the ears of his able henchman. His able hands smiled and left. What the criminal had whispered was the epitome of success for the near lands and that of the king's divine considerations as per his commandment. He had commanded his finest henchmen the *"black coats"*, the hooded assassins, most prolific murderous souls, to gather for his addressing, at his hideout by the pier. He had also directed one of his henchmen to recruit farmland hands to chop the finest wood for the captain's ships, ships of zeal and ones ready for conquest.

The captain and his royal confidant arrived at their destination, finally, they dismounted their horses and stepped onwards to his pier, one which was always his, for the mighty captain to operate and maneuver ships at his disposal, his beloved seafarer, the first mate ran towards him with a smile broader than sunlight. The captain embraced him with love and whispered in his ears. The shipman muttered slowly, "But my lord, I apologize, we just have four able ships, which I have made sure of that they are fit for a sea-bound adventure. Your ask is rather optimistic, O great admiral of the high seas".

The infamous criminal's henchmen appeared out of nowhere with mahogany planks and firmly cut wood and finally one of them glared, "My dear captain, commiserations from the master of crime, we have enough wood for thirteen odd ships for a fleet, the biggest these lands have ever seen and that of the far lands combined; allow us to help you with your shipyard enterprise, our commander directs us to fulfill your dreams". The captain shed a happy tear, one in harmony and of affirmation. He took a deep breath and glared, "let them through, let them help us in our auspicious endeavor; now get to work you all, hard to starboard!" The reinforced crew manned by the minister of interior, also the first mate and that of the finest henchmen of the mighty criminal, started the industrious endeavor of the most divine precedence, the work to overhaul the pride of the near lands.

The king was in royal melancholy, he asked his royal escorts to leave his proximity and also directed his cello player to rest for the day. He was in peace, his majesty knew exactly, that the affairs of his state were progressing with utmost enthusiasm and respect for the continuity of grandeur of the vast kingdom. He eventually retired for the day alone, after excusing himself from the heavenly presence of the moon gods. He ordered his servant to get a bottle of the finest wine of thy lands and his ardent servant got it ready at once.

He finally smiled and spoke politely with empirical congruity to his serviceman, "O my dear lad, for how long shall you run around and fulfill my words, come here sit with me and enjoy the night, let me pour you some good wine, let us cherish the moment before it's over and I am afloat a mighty ship bound to the infamous far lands". His servant was taken aback at such noble but an unusual gesture, "My lord, this is extremely kind of you, but may I remind you, I have served your father, the old king and never has it ever occurred a situation like this, where a servant is to adore royal precedence and relax with the king himself, my dear majesty, pardon me, I shall always decline such offers of prestige yet improbable kind, your honor".

The king let out lavish laughter and stated, "My dear lad, relax, you have served me and my old father well. You have made sure we are well pampered, taken care of without question, you, my lad deserve more than a drink with me, come sit with me and let me pour you a drink". The royal servant was astonished yet he dared not to disobey his master and sat near him. The king drew out two large portions of wine and served his royal aide with one. For the next hour they savored the fine wine without malice or insubordination. Just like old friends longing for a good life and great chatter. They were happy beyond belief.

Soon out of nowhere a hooded yet special henchman of the criminal approached the proximity of the chambers without the notice of the royal guards and bowed in front of the duo, at the utter bewilderment of the majesty's servants. The unknown adversary went ahead and revealed the progress of the legends with utmost pleasure and forbearing, "My lord, my Liege, my dear majesty of the near lands, my master has commanded me to relay this message to you without failure and at the earliest, the progress of the activities at the shipyard is going on smoothly and we shall be able to achieve the target of seventeen sea bearing ships, all ready, by four days from now, that is all but what I have your majesty". He bowed and evaporated into thin air, away from questions and the existence of the royal escapade.

The king was in celestial harmony of the notion for continuity and relevance of positive strategic implications for the path of glory which he and two beloved friends had chosen. He trotted into the royal pool with the confidence of a gladiator and dispersed his escorts again for the second time in his life. Only the cello player remained and was he found playing a far lands gypsy note, a muse which resonated so dear and real in terms of the situation on hand.

His servant poured the finest red wine into his glass and he cherished every sip of it with grandeur. Finally he asked his cello player to play his father's favorite tune, the "*old monarch*" it was called. The old musician was taken aback by the request yet he responded by the eternal melody of it. It was a show of musical connotation of the utmost purity. It tore into the great king's mind and he saw his state with clarity and finally understood his position, the position of utmost relevance. He was the king and responsibility ultimately knocked on his doors for eternal enlightenment, mental clarity of the understanding of the reality of the kingdom and its governance. He stood in front of the pool of royal waters, walked towards the musician, hugged him dearly then scampered towards his chambers. Once in, he ordered his servant to fetch another bottle of the finest wine of the lands. Finally he poured it into his royal glass and the king politely asked his servant to fetch for the cello player. The servant obeyed his master's command at once.

Soon the old musician was found in the king's royal yet homely surroundings. Obliged was he, heart beating at an exaggerated pace, sweat glands shedding its ominous tears, worried to death. The king stood and hugged him again, kissed him and poured some good wine in another glass, finally handing it to his fine musician. The shocked old cello player accepted his king's gestures of uncertain yet awkward kindness with a feather of doubt but did not pursue any unnecessary questioning. The king let out a huge sigh and proclaimed his thoughts, raw it was but significant for the occasion. He stated, " My good friend, you have served my father, myself, unfortunately, I do not have any lineage following me yet but I adore you for your act of humane kindness towards such nimble yet royal souls as that of my father and the unfortunate yet surviving hierarchy, that is me. Thank you my friend, your music has enlightened me beyond conviction".

The old cello player burst out into tears, which obviously could fill a small lagoon, rather a river. He blabbered with dignity and elation of the highest kind, "My lord, My Liege, my majesty, you are too kind to speak on my behalf and too considerate to adore a mere cello player trying to meet his bestowed needs on his workday, but you are more than the right to say about your father enjoying my musical composition, which unfortunately you did not for a longer period than I had expected. But you finally did, apologies my master for highlighting, but I know how you are but mightier than your predecessor and eminent ancestor". With great passion he added, "You, my lord is a visionary, like that of your father, reborn to see us to greater glory and you are your father's son, Amen".

They both hugged in consensus, and embraced delivering a statement of honor and belonging so definite and resolute that there was finally faith within commoners and royals in near lands. The artiste finished his drink, bowed and left with a grandiose smile. The king perceived a knocking sound on his royal windows, one on his royal window panes. He stood and opened his palatial window panes and smiled at the hiero-falcon, waiting on his window sills. He let it trot in and patted its back. He spoke in a royal nature, "My dear governor I know why you have come, I believe you my honorable friend of a friend, that of my dearest captain's, the mighty one, the master of the high seas is progressing just fine as expected and you come to portray, rather relay your legends message, pour out his mind filled with vision and security for the greatness of the kingdom, is it not true, tell me O great bird".

The hiero-falcon let out a humongous chirp and sat at the king's right shoulder. A cognizant statement to uphold his master's deeds and gratitude for another human who understood this undertaking of importance yet great devotion for the betterment of the kingdom, the kingdom of hope. The mighty bird flew and sat on the royal desk of the king, to nibble at a few hazelnuts destined for him. The king took a deep breath in the gratification of the progress and fortified rejuvenation of the days which had empowered him and the kingdom beyond doubt.

The days had pronounced the lands, the best lands to live in. He slipped into his royal bed in slumber and found himself in a state of subconsciousness, a dreamland filled with harmonious drama. His favorite people were there, all of them, his secret yet red adversary, his favorite cello player, his two legendary friends, the bird, the interior minister, his servant, his favorite whore, yet there was another man unknown. The moon god was in-evident and hiding was he, the stars were not present too, the darkness besieged the atmosphere with the ingenuity of fulfillment as prescribed by the gods. And silence engulfed the lands and that of the high seas.

In the morning, a morning brightened by the Sun god's grace and his heavenly warmth, the two legends stood by the king's bed adoring the view of his majesty in slumber with a smile written all over his facial contour. The captain winked at the criminal to pester the mighty king out of his repose. The criminal swiftly sat beside the king and played with his ears, of course with a feather of pigeon's descent. The king finally shrugged his dream fairy off and opened his graceful eyes to embrace it upon his two dearest confidants, by his side. He stood and hugged them no questions asked, cause he knew, all was but settled for the providence of glory to sustain and the logistics for the extraordinary expedition planned and dealt with. The trio smiled and the captain led the way out of the chambers.

Dawn it was, one of a kind, the glitter was extraordinaire, nature still all but bowing in front of the legends to pass across the royal escapade uninterrupted. Soon they were at the gates and three magnificent horses waiting to carry them, when they please, to traverse across to their destination. They boarded their magnificent beasts and the criminal nodded, then rode eastward, the duo followed with intrigue and blissful conformity of positivity beaming in their faces.

In a flash they were in front of the criminal's favored hideout and twenty-four hooded men stood in attention before them. The scene was serene yet gratifying, with a sense of utmost security. The criminal dismounted his horse and now stood in between his friends and that of his sleuths, them masterful legion of spies. He glared at them with purpose, "Comrades, brothers in arms, are you ready for the new proposition for the retribution of glory and peace of the near lands?"

The congregation of spies added in a unified yet bone-chilling note, "Yes master, your command is our desire, your direction our life, we will penetrate the seas when it is asked for and that of the far-lands. We shall see to that our goal is but concluded with victory carved all over it, Amen".

The trio shook each hooded man's hand in pride and hugged each one of them, for gratification and goodness for the kingdom. Finally the king declared, "My dear soldiers of these lands, the finest sleuths, soldiers unknown yet present, I command you to be true to thy master, the infamous criminal and fulfill all duties of the kingdom as preached, Amen".

The seagulls hovered over them in tranquility, the legends embraced in zeal with the future intact and destiny sealed, the Gods beamed and the wind god played a serene orchestra, chilly enough to mark the start of an insinuating yet intimidating exposure of greatness, an expedition beyond belief.

--------------------------------------XXXXXXXXXXXXXXX--

10. The Expedition

"Time walks, time runs, time flies, there is but no time for time. Sometimes time is money, sometimes it is of the essence, but this time around, the feeling for the time was quite peculiar for the legendary trio. The angelic druid gave his narration a pause when a thick mass of cloud passed through in between him and the man in white. Once the coast was clear he continued his divine prophecy....."

A few days had passed, then suddenly one of the criminal's finest henchmen appeared in the royal chambers out of the blue and smiled at the king and bowed. The king smiled back and followed his mysterious visitor out unto the courtyard.

Soon they were on horseback, riding hastily towards the near lands promenade. Finally after a brief sprint on horseback, they reached their primal destination. The captain and the criminal were there, they waved at their friend in intrinsic excitement and the king trotted towards them. They were together again. This was when time stopped. It was rather their unified feeling to behold, of course. But for them it did stop. The panorama ahead was ceremonious and incomparably unbelievable.

The captain's hands, the criminal's finest henchmen, the interior minister's loyal guards had achieved something of greatness, it was an astonishing achievement in such a short span of time, even time seemed shocked and took notice. Seventeen magnificent ships were standing tall and bestowed consensus of natural desire and that of the grandeur of the near lands at the naval pier.

In utter shock the King muttered, "How on earth did this happen, my dear captain". The captain understanding his master and his confused words, and of course his state of mind, declared, "Do not underestimate the skills at our disposal in them near lands my lord, I had four ships of my own left after the drastic affairs of our last voyage, the other thirteen ships were built by that of zeal, the confidence and the brute force of probability by our assorted hands at our disposal, what do you think of our fleet now my grace?".

The king declared blissfully and the time god ticked in reality again, "Marvelous, this is beyond imagination, let us besiege upon them high seas and that of the lands afar, before this week ends, I command and thank you both for overseeing such an improbable task with such precision and in such a short a time frame". The trio hugged and left for the royal chambers. On the way they nodded in appreciation towards the interior minister, who nodded back to certify the greatest of efforts dealt on the task on hand and the accomplishment of pure camaraderie enforced righteously by the legends.

The sun gods played along and shone bright rays of light to adore them ships, the ships they glittered, so did the souls who built them. Everyone was ecstatic, even time was. The winds responded in the utmost favorable manner when the trio reached the royal courtyard.

The captain jumped out of his horse and felt the mild gale, finally smiling in eternal concord. The two legends now slowly crept behind the back of the mighty captain and quizzically examined him. They peered on from each side at the captain. The master seafarer was on his own muse, devoid of the fact that his two best mates were on his side, examining him in detail, as a guinea pig on fodder, for examination. The muse of the mighty seafarer continued and the shape of the westerlies curving and kissing him off his cheeks, reminded him of the good old days. The hard yet floating days of freedom and hardship.

Then he smiled and opened his eyes and addressed his two constant examiners, " My friends the rare westerly gale is forming, when it starts, it stays, at least for half a month, and it blows from across the near lands towards the far lands shore, a gale which on each growing day becomes mightier, stronger and if you have it on your back, one shall be hitting the far lands shore before it bid farewell for this moon year, I suggest your majesty we set sail without fail, at first light tomorrow morning".

The king looked at the criminal, who nodded in affirmation and decisively his majesty glared out loud, " I concur my friend, let the show begin". The two friends of the indomitable near lands King now took a quick bow and left to make eminent preparations for the day ahead. The king had a wry smile on his face when he strode with his head held high towards the royal chambers. He knew, the nature around too, so did the atmosphere, the gods, that the eternal commandment for a grand conquest has been triggered. And it was just time, to embrace the glory of the most epic proportions.

The sun gods bowed in harmony, the darkness set in, slowly the moon god took command of the heavenly vigil and shed necessary light at the rush of affairs ongoing in the near lands naval promenade. The atmosphere was alive and so was the humane effort in them piers. The activity was at its utmost primal state, henchmen running around to make strategic ends meet in terms of stability and execution of the final goal, a goal so true and pure. One which each individual present in the nearshore pier, toiled and devoted their *"today"* for.

The seagulls were but mere spectators, now grounded on land observing closely with an air of wonder and zeal at the magnanimous proceedings, to make the ship's sea ready. The westerlies saw an occasion for the attainment of credibility and excitement of adventurous precedence, hence upgrading their gale-force up a notch to make their presence felt and hardworking humane hearts filled with overjoyed enthusiasm to complete the colossal task at hand.

The evolution of the breeze to a gale and of the day skies to that of the starry nights, the progression towards a stark, dull darkness of a hood so clean, the dusky ivory was just an epic phenomena to behold. The king found himself awake right before the first light. He hassled to find his proper clothing for the occasion and picked his majestic sword for the matter on hand. He was ready when the two primal legends, his best mates, entered his chambers, all in smiles. Warm hugs of gratitude and passion ensued and the sun gods authorized the moment by peering an eye to shed special light rays of appreciation.

The fabled trio, now all geared up for the adventure, advanced towards the three stallions, awaiting their gracious mount, in front of the courtroom in the royal courtyard. The solo cello player played the tune to behold, one heart-piercing musical fantasy it was, a muse to worship and pay respect and homage to the parting avengers of freedom, recognition and hope. A hope for the victory in foreign lands, a hope so pure, so true, one which engulfed the entire sovereign and basked in the wee morning light for its eternal existential recognition.

Soon the legends galloped through the heart of the near lands, where commoners stood on the roadside as if they were highlighting to the pathway unto the navy piers. The nation's legends were greeted all along their inland journey, with humongous cheers for good luck "*bon voyage, Godspeed*", them screamed, the citizens with great pride, them clapped out loud. It was as if one of their own sons had taken upon this colossal task to secure the glory of the near lands.

Finally the legends reached their destined spot near the naval promenade. The king was in a divine melancholy, words missed his royal mouth, he still could not believe what he saw. The near lands fleet was ready and able seamen standing in attention on each magnificent deck. All seventeen ships now stood anchored, ready for the adventure and perils of the epic voyage, which beckoned.

The minister of interior approached the trio filled with pride. With a smile on his face he gleamed, "My dear majesty, O just king, all is well and the ships well-tuned for a farce at sea and beyond". He took a sublime bow. The king jumped out of his horse unto the ground and embraced him with a tight yet warm hug and declared, "My dear minister, you have served my father, the old king and have done volumes for my sustenance in governing this special kingdom, our home, I hereby declare you the deserved position, you are now the *"king's hand"*, you shall faithfully govern these lands whence I am seaborne, you shall run all affairs of the state by your noble judgement, until I return, I pray, fail me not my lad".

The newly appointed '*king's hand*' took a grandiose bow and bend a knee in divine respect and acceptance of the royal notion. He finally stated with glaring pride, " O mighty king, the ruler of this lands, I humbly obey your command, I bid you farewell and safe return, of course, good luck and Godspeed in your industrious yet challenging endeavor. With a heavy heart tears flowing slowly, tears of joy, holding the king's hand he further added, " Bon Voyage, my Lord, your stronghold awaits you for your imminent return, hope you shall attain sea victory and beyond".

The king accredited his minister's graceful words with a pat on his back and progressed towards the captain's finest ship. One which the mighty seafarer had always commanded. One which was nearest to the pier, one which had seen life, death, victory, defeat, joy, yet it was the hope which it cherished, so did the denizens of the near lands, a belief in the heavenly propositions of hope of the purest kind. The criminal's finest yet hooded sleuths had assembled somewhat like a formation of a platoon so niche and stood in astute attention near the end of the pier next to the ship. The trio had reached them and soon the master sleuths took a bow and with each knee bent, they glared in a union, "long live thy legends of the near lands, long live thy king, we shall be a part of your historically dynamic journey of conquest and more, we shall serve you with our lives, thy lord".

The king smiled at the criminal and the feeling was mutual, as the master of the sleuths nodded towards them to board the magnanimous ship. The sleuths were on deck, so were the legends of legends. The captain took his position on deck, and then the admiralty ordered the men to scatter and divided the tasks to proceed with lifting the anchor. He stood tall near his cabin and glared out loud, "Ahoy! All ships set sail, anchors up, Bosun's to man their position at the bow helm, full sails drawn, I command".

The captain's first mate echoed his master's orders and it was obeyed instantaneously throughout in union. Able seamen hustled on board, the hustle bustle and somber tussle continued and to echo their positive musical notions the royal orchestra now onboard, hummed a tune, an adventurous one. The criminal and his majesty, the king leaned on the railings that of the starboard side and enjoyed the vastness of the high seas bashing against the ship in the morning sun. The excited westerlies kissed their sun-drenched faces to welcome their presence in the high seas.

The lead vessel, the captain's own, took center stage, followed by the entire fleet in an arrowhead formation. Out of the pristine blue sky, in came flying, the hiero-falcon and landed on its master's shoulders. The captain patted its back and strolled onwards to join the king and the criminal. Once again the trio stood in unity on deck, the captain looked at his falcon and stated, "O magnificent bird, the almighty eyes, the task on hand this time around is sacred and of the utmost urgent kind, go my dear friend and report to me immediately if you see any prey of the humankind, afloat in the waters between the two infamous landmasses, I pray, fail me not since there is no room for failure this time around".

The omnipotent yet real governor of the high seas, the hiero-falcon obeyed his master's command, he hooted out loud in corroboration of the commandment and flew out high, on towards the northeastern sky to mark the commencement of a voyage so dear to the near lands. The captain led his friends to the port side where a large table made of the finest mahogany was placed, along with three large chairs, almost resembling thrones of the royals. They sat there to enjoy the westerlies and the passing seagulls, to adore the stark blue waters and the never-ending skies, waves dashing against other waves, small and big shoals of fine fish swimming around in this eternal harmony.

The captain's first mate approached him, seasoned seafarer he was, the finest seaman on his master's reporting. He wanted to know on his further orders for the high noon to approach. The captain nodded at his favorite seaman and uttered," My good lad, set course to the northeast, full speed ahead, I pray, also please do let the master chef know that we would like to have the finest port wine and the best fresh catch for the day to be served for our lunch today, thank you, that would be all". The first mate took a bow and disappeared in a flash to set sails as directed and on his way informed the master chef on board to make preparations for the seaborne luncheon of the legends.

The Bosun had made sure the captain's wheels pointed in the desired direction and the mainmast was now fully cast out to entertain the westerlies and in turn gain maximal speed on the occasion. The lead vessel traversed swiftly through the serene high seas like a knife through molten butter. A seafarer was now evident on the helm of the ship, with a harpoon, aiming was he for a few passing shoals of swordfish, fine meat they carry. After a while of patience and wait, a harpoon flashed across the port side, right into the pristine clear waters of the high seas, the struggle was mammoth. But finally, the able seafarer was able to haul aboard a huge swordfish, of course, followed by eminent praise of the three legends. The captain was impressed and hence glared out loud, "Fine catch my lad, steady hands mate, and good luck for more".

Soon a dozen more kills were hauled overboard, fish of vivid variety they were, sharks, mullets, tuna and more. It was quite a fascinating exhibition for the king and the criminal, who were but for the first time in their lives, been seaborne. They clapped in joy, commended the able hand on his prized catches for the day and sat back on their position on the port side.

Soon another seafarer, the cook's mate, bought in the finest port wine and poured out three glasses full, up to the brim. Glasses clanked, merry was the mood aboard the lead carrier. The legends basked in the high noon glory with fine wine, some laughter and of course tales of glory to come. The orchestra followed the happy mood and played a similar muse. A muse so glad, it made the king dance in utter elation. The chef and his mate approached the legends with their afternoon luncheon. Grand it was, a feast to behold, they served the fabled trio, a portion each of smoked swordfish garnished with olives and tease of lemon, along with a dash of salt to make it perfect in taste. The aroma filled the deck, and the hungry legends thanked the master chef and in turn devoured their meal in a flash.

The king was satisfied, his belly content, finally taking a huge gulp of the fine wine, "Marvelous lunch this is, a lunch at sea, how very peacefully serene, how excellent a meal, life at the high seas is but just perfect, my dear captain". The captain let out a mocking laugh and retorted, "My Lord, make no such mistakes of trusting the sea, time and tide await none, the westerlies are infamous for their devastation at sea, lucky are we who have it on our backs, moreover there are situations when the hunter gets hunted in these sacred waters, I pray, trust your instincts at all times".

The king commended the captain for his intelligent words and parted to his cabin for an afternoon nap. The criminal also retired with a high note to rest for a while, towards his quarters. The captain went to his favorite cabin and laid on his back smiling at the situation, he was back at sea again, once again the prospect of guts and glory beckoned. More gold to gather, them lands to conquer. He was at peace, a peace of mind and that of the soul. The trio was now momentarily separated. Soon they fell into a convoluted dream world. One in which they found each other, in a master's stroke of telepathy, confirming the situation that they were but inseparable. Undeniably in a union they were, for a cause so greater than themselves, even that of conquest and beyond.

They found themselves together in the magnificent beaches of the far lands, a sudden breeze of the easterly winds pushed them backwards and they turned back towards their ships and could count only twelve of them afloat. Quizzically exchanging glances they moved on and soon came upon a limitless stretch of sunflower cultivation, they decided to traverse across it. For some uncertain reason the orchestra now played a note of confusion and growing curiosity, a tune apt for a cat and mouse encounter. They pried on across the cultivation in melancholy yet filled with uncertainty of the outcome to the brim. Soon they were mounting over a small hillock when a group of masked assassins circled them. Then they were dragged on to a dingy yet mammoth dungeon, a prisoner's nightmare it was and the padlock clanked out loud, to declare the conformity of their state of imprisonment.

The three legends woke up in a state of shock, from this eventful, short yet malicious nightmare, rather a *day-mare* of exquisite intrigue and tragedy. This dreamful event was immediately followed by a large scream from the Captain's treasured seaman, the first mate, one that was made in realistic circumstances. The Captain leaped out, so did the other two legends and they rushed to the main deck for an extended report and of course for the realization of reality.

The skies were gloomy, the sun god absent. Heavy clouds had barred his proclamation of existence, the westerlies had an invisible cunning smile worn on the gale, which made it tough to walk without support on deck. The scene was set for thunder to reclaim his ordinance and let his rage govern the incoming evening. The captain met his first mate on the way, who seemed troubled, and he saw fear in his eyes for the first time in many moon years. The captain put a hand to his worried shoulders with an essence to portray his calmness and with prime eyes looked at his esteemed seafarer. The first mate took a deep breath, the king and the criminal now joined the duo on the central stage.

The seasoned seafarer finally uttered with great urgency, "O mighty captain, the weather had deteriorated and the Bosun saw seven ships, them that of the far lands, off the horizon before the lights faded. There might be more, and due to the current conditions we are but blind my lord!" The captain's most cherished bird, the hiero falcon flew out of the darkness, up onto his shoulders and started hooting out loud, he glared nine times.

The captain smiled and resounded his dearest friend's intricate report out loud, "My dear friends, my finest able hands of the high-seas, masterful sleuths of the great criminal, there are but nine ships of the far lands approaching. And going by my instincts and directive of my beloved eyes I believe we have enough time to strategize a convoluted plan to usurp whatever they carry and demolish their presence. I mean war my friends, war at sea, now more than ever, are you with me, tell me, are you? "The king, criminal and the entire plethora of humane existence boomed in a union, "Yes master, ahoy! Governor of the high seas, your order is our command!"

Expeditious were they, the consortium of henchmen under the captain's command, up to the task for a seaborne conquest. In a flash they took upon their souls to resort to the unanimous confirmation, the affirmation of their master's order, hustling were they to make ends meet. The able seaman, the first mate darted towards the stern with a lamp and started to wave it in a peculiar rhythm. The captain smiled, the two legends along with him looked at the affair quizzically in utter confusion. The captain saw convolution of thoughts in the eyes of his two legendary associates and stated to keep them at ease, "Oh guess what, my favorite henchman is up to, he is warning the others, of the incoming ships and the time for battle stations to commence in the appropriate hour, this is how we get ready for many a duel, we have fought in these high seas".

He further added, "You see my friends, in the sea, even if we are blinded by the dusk and the fog until the last moment; navigation and cartography matters the most and of course trust, I trust my Bosun more than myself and also my first mate's fear of the unknown. But them far lands fighter ships are outnumbered and they know it too, it's just time now, which shall tell the reality of the outcome. That is whether they want to engage or not, but my dear lords, either way, I heard nine and nine I shall devour; you see I cannot let down my repertoire at the high seas". With these words the captain let out a burst of humongous laughter, his golden fore teeth glittering in the now starry night.

After a moment of stillness as directed by the captain to all humans on board, the ship trotted through the dense fog which was now setting in. The moon gods shedding his torch of nightly direction to help see a few notches ahead at the least. Uncertainty besieged the fleet, dazed and muted in union were they, just like the whisper of death. The captain had also commanded his first mate to go dead slow and to maintain formation, moreover, he had asked to relay the same to the others and his message was instantaneously delivered.

The criminal's sleuths drew their swords, so did the king. The Bosun sitting atop the main mass now saw a positive glimmer of light and quickly traversed down on the deck to inform. He hurried towards the captain and whispered with a sense of utmost urgency in his ears and ran back down to grab a sword from the armory in the hold.

The captain was at the forefront of all enthralling drama. He jumped on to the ropes of the mainmast like an orangutan and held and swerved like a pole dancer, surveying the immediate horizon intricately. He looked back and smiled and signaled, "Three", "four", "two", with his fingers in quick succession. His favorite seaman his first mate understood his mater's depiction of the change in far land's fleet formation. He ran back towards the stern and relayed the message promptly. The captain was in a thought so deep, one which passed in a flash with respect to time and action for the forbearing development. He smiled again whence he had the answers to the seafaring problem, he repeated his coded dramatic response and relayed his decision on the near land's best formation to engage. He held a, "five", "seven", and finally another "five", with his fingers. The first mate repeated his smirk and flashed back to the stern to relay the commandment and relay he did, similar to other numerous occasions, with a flickering lamp waving in the thick seaborne air.

The Bosun was back on deck, the captain retreated to meet him, had a quick whisper of the proposed course of action to take place in the immediate near future. The Bosun smiled and waved for the finest henchmen that of the criminals and of course the able seamen at disposal to regroup closely, so that he could direct them on the plan of plunder. A plan so intricate to overthrow a boat filled to the brim within a few moments, a structured approach to high seas battle.

The Bosun whispered, it sounded like hoarse thunder, he started to get ready for the upcoming impact, how to devour through the first wave of assassins and quickly make a dash for the hold, which but held treasure, treasure pure and great. He devised an act that pushes the first wave of assassins to retract and get segregated in the process to manage the assault, yet get confused in their priority of safeguarding their ship. The consortium of henchmen and able seamen acknowledged with an appropriate nod of their heads for their acceptance of greater good.

The king smiled, so did the criminal in union and in conformity of this strategic concourse set in place. The Bosun rushed atop the mainmast, a position of importance. The entire crew acted in union to the divine directive and prepared for impact.

Silence prevailed, before the storm, and the enemy ships appeared. The captain turned the wheels to maneuver the ship so that the impact was side-on, a starboard side impact was what all able seafarers cherished. The plot was thick yet it was set for the mammoth vengeance to be delivered with righteous retribution.

The captain glared out loud, "Lock ships and prepare for combat". The first ship now clanked with the majestic ship of the old seafarer. As directed by the visionary director of the high seas, ropes flew and the plethora of hands on deck jumped overboard to conquer the enemy vessel.

The king along with the criminal glared a mammoth war cry, "Kill at will! Let us devour them downtrodden mongrels". The far-lands fighters were all taken aback at such precision of sea-bound combat procedures, yet they fought on bravely. The captain was seen flashing his blade around and blood and heads splattered on deck. He growled like a mature lion. Out of the night sky in came his favorite bird and pounced upon a prey and tore an eye, for his late-night dinner. The criminal smiled in tandem, then thrusted his sleek blade into the heart of the far-land's captain. The remaining fighters were aghast beyond belief but continued their futile course of action, one without a leader. The criminal's sleuths added a finishing touché to such a voracious event by rapidly slitting enemy throats as if they were but meat for a grandiose luncheon.

The Bosun and the king progressed towards the hold of the ship where two fighters tried to stop them at their tracks. The king was late to react and his opponent flashed his blade at him, his majesty held it midair. Small trickles of royal blood dropped below onto the open spaces between the grills of the hold. With thy free hand, the hand which held the authoritative royal symbol of vengeance the sword, now moved and pierced his opponent's throat, killing him spontaneously.

The Bosun took a wild swivel of his blade at his opponent and found his enemy cut in half along with his weak blade broken on impact. The captain's most treasured seafarer, his first mate now joined the valiant company and with a mighty kick, knocked open the padlock, off the hold. All enemy souls had fallen, now it was loud and clear, that the hold remained theirs to devour. The captain nodded at the king and he nodded in turn.

The first mate and the Bosun reacted and lifted the grill, off the hold. Finally they peered below and entered. Another group now formed near the hold to await any signals of peril from below, in case any surprises broke out of the monstrous hold.

The Bosun glared, with a pressing voice, from the hold below, "Captain, my lord, dear master, I pray, can you come here and see what we found". The captain nodded at his fabled friends to join in as well and they obeyed the command of the grandmaster of the high seas. The trio now gradually traversed down into the hold in the hope to find the unknown. Once down below, they looked up and their jaws dropped out in union; at the sight which lay in front.

--XXXXXXXXXXXXXX--

11. Discovery of Eternal Love

"Love is but blind as them say, yet at times love blinds you eternally. When that happens, the blindness binds you in a pristine bond of togetherness, never known before, one which makes you see only one person before you and nothing else matters or exists, even in close proximity. Eyes locked seeking answers to questions never asked before. The heart creates an orchestra of its own, beating its drums so hard, it knows not why such a phenomena started. A smile is finally let out followed by that of the other human and finally the conformity and establishment of the divine happiness, of the essence of love is realized."

Similar was the situation in the dimly lit hold of the far lands fighter ship. Three pairs of eyes locked in eternal harmony, searching for longlines and uncharted destiny. The king's natural eyes were locked on to a pair of hazelnut oculus of a demigoddess, a beauty never perceived before, one to behold. Their eyes were smiling and then they started talking in tandem.

The captain was busy engaging his marvelous stare at the brunette with ivory eyes. The criminal had found a foxy lady who was winking at him and he froze to examine her stark green eyes, an effort or a situation which had never been so important, one which has never been entrusted upon him to fulfill or foresee.

The Bosun and the first mate exchanged glances quizzically. The seasoned seamen were worried and confused, whether their masters were interested in the loot or the femme Fatales discovered in the hold. To break the everlasting silence created by the celestial romance of the highest kind, the first mate evaded their royal privy and uttered, "Ahem, dear guvnor, my captain, kindly advice on the probable course of action for the safekeeping of the gains, eh My Lord".

The governor of the high seas woke up from his romantic yet divine semi-slumber and stammered, "Yes, oh yes, I mean, yeah, my lad, what was I thinking, two of you await my orders on deck, let me gather my thoughts on the transfer of the cargo, why don't you two gather a small troop to secure the gains back to the ship, I shall call upon you once I am done thinking, I pray".

The Bosun and the first mate let out a mocking smile at their master, perceiving his situation and his sheer plight of misery at such a remote feeling. On their way out they patted his shoulders, the captain made a quizzical expression but smiled back at the female goddess in front of him in an apologetic manner, as if he had committed a heinous crime.

Silence prevailed for a gasp of time, then finally the criminal broke the ice and probed, "Dear lovely ladies, kindly describe your presence in this hold, and of course the fact about where you are from and who imprisoned you". The king thwarted before anyone could, " Pardon my dear friend for his query, I guess that can be answered at a later time when you three see fit and especially when you are free from this dingy hold, I pray, kindly follow us upstairs onto the deck".

The hazelnut eyed, demi goddess spoke, and when she spoke the king almost had a cardiac arrest. The femme fatale added, " My Good Lord, on the contrary, I would like to answer the question posed by your dear friend, since the knowledge is but deserved, and in order to start compensating for your debts of kindness to free us from this treacherous holding, this would be our first step in the right direction, I believe".

The captain couldn't handle his overbearing excitement as always and blared, " Dear lady, who is that conniving soul who imprisoned you three in such a pathetic hold, tell me, I shall pounce upon them scoundrels at once and bury them in these deep waters, I promise you, Mi lady".

The king intervened with the utmost politeness, "My Love, don't mind the mighty captain, he is but extremely concerned at your plight and revenge is brewing in his veins, I pray, please continue your story, since this may shed some light to the situation, post which I the near lands king, shall promise you and your friends safety and prosperity for moon years ahead".

The hazelnut eyed princess, shed a tear and took a bow, in front of the just king and finally, she stated, " Dear Majesty, your highness, you are but too cordial a soul and so are your companions who joined you in this seaborne exercise, I wish I shall be able to recompense your kindness, thanks a lot for saving me and my dear sisters, we are but the princesses of them far off lands, them lands that lay beyond the far lands, we were on a fishing trip with our father, the king, when a ravenous far lands fighter ship, the one we stand upon now, attacked us, killed our dear father, looted our belongings and imprisoned us to be delivered as royal escorts, as gifts to the cunning far lands king".

The legendary trio was now boiling with vengeance, they exchanged glances. The king broke the sadness borne silence and added," Pardon our ignorance dear princess and please there is but nothing to repay us for, we are but just simple folks of them near lands, we shall definitely "by Jove", take revenge for your loss; to make it more crystal, we do have a long-standing cause for retribution and conquest of them far lands, we are on a sea-borne expedition to sow calmness, governance and eventually justice for a fair share of freedom to live and to prosper, apologies again for dragging this conversation at length, we can converse later, I would request that the three of us escort you to our mighty ship of my dear captain".

With a deep satisfactory gasp of air he further continued," Moreover, you pretty ladies must be tormented, tired and bored at being kept in such a tiny hole at length. It's but too unkind to prolong your freedom. Please, may I lead you upstairs onto the deck?" The king let out a hand and bowed, the princess immediately smiled and took his hand without any fear. Happiness engulfed her, and was she blown away by the king's charming yet charitable proposition.

The king nodded at his legendary friends, who woke up from their heavenly slumber. Distracted were they by the angelic beauties so far but now stood to follow the king's order. They too bowed and let out a hand towards their favorite ladies.

The two other archduchesses also responded humbly, with a twinkle of faith in their beautiful eyes, finally they grab them hands gracefully. The captain now locked his stare on the pure set of ivory eyes in front and smiled. The king was already in heaven at the sight in front, the criminal was flying high yet he managed to utter a few words, "Dear majesty, kindly lead the way, I pray, its but getting hot in here, ventilation is minimal I suppose". Sweating was he with the warmth of them hands, that of the femme fatale in front of him. The small troupe now understood the hidden sarcasm and laughed out loud and finally the king nodded. He led the way out holding the *"damsel in distress"*, the one with the hazelnut eyes. Soon the captain and the criminal followed with their damsels, on towards the main deck of the fallen ship.

Urgent but subdued murmurs ran on deck, ones between the Bosun and that of his first mate. Soiled and seasoned seafarers, a sea bearing mechanism to oversee any of the mighty captain's high seas façade, they were. They got into a deep conversation, filled to the brim with sarcasm and that of intrigue. The Bosun asked the captain's favorite seafarer, " Oi Ol hands, I sniff a rat, the guvnor is a tad bit under the weather I presume, tell me am I right mate, never seen him in such a faltering state after winning a ship brother". The first mate jeered in a sarcastic manner, "Ye you are right brother, I guess it's not the weather but the bug, the nasty little predator, I feel he is done for, our good captain".

The Bosun had a bewildered yet comic look of understanding. He added, " Knew it, he's been bitten, holy Moses, here we go, them arise, I can hear noises, let's be cautious you never know them *"damsels in distress"* might have overpowered our naïve and fragile near lands souls and captured them at ransom". The first mate let out an epic smile and drew out his cutlass. He retorted with forbearing pleasures, "I agree to disagree, but as you say My dear friend, caution is good for health and longevity when we embrace such times". The Bosun drew out his long sword and nodded in acknowledgement. Spooked were they at such uncanny behavior portrayed by the captain, worried they were since their master had never witnessed love or ever had the opportunity to express such emotions.

The trio now slowly appeared on deck, one by one, flanked by them, demi goddesses. The entire raving deck went on an infinite silence in a flash at the panorama of events unfolding in front of them. It was as if the entire crew had a heart attack, observing their master the infamous captain, flanked by a beauty. The Bosun awkwardly stood in front of this heavenly façade and he looked back at the first mate in awe of the situation, and the first mate gave him a stern look. Which of course he obeyed with utter intrigue, "Long live the king, long live the legends of thy near lands, Ahem, make way for his majesty, get the planks ready".

The entirety of the crew reverberated the bosun's praise in a union, "Long live thy king, long live the legends, long live near lands". The first mate silently led the special troupe towards the planks for a traversal on towards the captain's ship. Another seafarer interrupted their advance. Huffing and puffing for air was he, finally he uttered looking towards the captain, "Ahoy Guvnor, the entire far lands fleet of nine able ships has been captured and recovery of gains and that's of gold is in progress, My Lord, all henchmen aboard shall wait for your command for eminent future actions".

He took a bow, quizzically looked at the captain and almost got a heart attack at the sight of him holding a lady in one hand. He finally muttered looking at the first mate, "Eh, is everything all right Sire". The first mate gave him a look of the "God of Death", glaring at him with red eyes.

The poor seafarer died on the spot virtually at them vengeance filled eyes focused at him. The irony continued on board and the demi goddesses smirked and finally let out a chuckle at the rusty comedy on deck. The now red-faced captain understanding the benevolent trolls of his seafaring mates now finally declared, " My good lad, Thank you for such great news at the righteous hour, I promote you hereby to be the Bosun of my ship and of course our dear Ol' Bosun has been promoted to a rather empty seat on deck, "the second mate". The ex-Bosun, now the second mate had a brain fade and walked towards the captain and whispered in his ears, "Thank you my lord but are you sure Guvnor". The captain smiled and nodded at him, and finally kissed him.

The now second mate fell on deck instantaneously, drawing funny jeers all-around deck and that of the near lands fleet, who now observed the scenes with their field glasses all directed towards the drama on the far-lands ship's deck. Sarcastic it was, the fall of the second mate smiling in repose, the trio flanked by the damsels now advanced again, when the captain looked back at the newly appointed Bosun, who was in a world of utter shock. The captain finally declared, "My lad make sure all them gains are well secured in the safety of our holds, make merry until noon tomorrow, I will command later, on our next course of action soon".

He nodded towards the first mate who bowed and stood in obedience and the Bosun nodded, finally running towards the stern of the ship to relay the god-fearing message. One which governs all in that of the high seas, the captain's commandment for the day. The king successfully traversed along with the hazel-eyed princess with minimal support from the first mate.

The criminal followed next with his *"damsel in no longer distress"*, all but in smiles in divine union, onto the captain's lead ship. Finally it was the captain's turn and that of his lady in arms. They were about to cross them planks overboard to his ship, when the first mate in a flash, closed in near the ears of the governor of the high seas and whispered, " Oi captain, the crew and I feel you have been bitten, take care my friend and good luck". The captain looked at him and the old friendly seafarer, his best mate was but all in smiles and the master of the high seas was all red, in embarrassment but had to laugh at the sarcastic atrocities posed by his seasoned seafaring mates. He nodded and almost ran towards safer quarters of his ship. Finally the trio was now on the port side, seated along with them demi goddesses, in the brilliant mahogany table.

The silence was broken by the magnificent musical harmony of the royal orchestra. Which played a unique yet frivolous and mysterious note of love, which was but heart rendering and touched the damsels and that of the trio at once. Eyes met, heart, throbbed, sweat poured, feeling shared in an autonomous fashion, without any distraction. In the deepest tranquil were, the three pairs. The king broke the eudemonic silence by muttering a few words, in a shy tone, "Dear ladies, let me do a quick introduction of me and my compatriots, our purpose as you already know, well I am the king, he is the infamous captain of them high seas, one whom I bet, you must have heard of at length and this over here is our good and most intelligent friend, "the criminal". He was of course a criminal once, now he assists us in our mission with the most immaculate strategic imperative and that of his brilliant intelligence, now if you may, mi ladies, kindly introduce yourselves".

The hazelnut eyed princess smiled and added at length, "Your majesty, I am *"Maria"*, that's my name". Pointing to the ivory eyed princess, her sister, she added, "That is my elder sister "Ella". Further glances towards the other side, on towards her other sister, with green eyes she declared, " And this is "Elta" my younger sister, on behalf of all of us we would like to thank you, three great humans, for saving us and granting us solace and shelter under your grandiose ship, I have to mention all three of you, do not need your introductions at all, you legends are but well-known in all of them lands; since we have heard your stories of brevity from travelling gypsies in one way or the other, it's an honor to meet you three in this lifetime and under such circumstances".

The criminal had a mysterious smile on his face yet he managed to utter a few kind words, "You thank us too much, my dear princess, your safety is but our duty, my dearest legendary friends also favor the same, good to know you dear princesses, hope we are altogether successful in our vision of achievement of the greater good, Amen".

The master seafarer was disturbed by the sudden arrival of his favorite bird, who flew in, to sit on his shoulders. The captain smiled at it and looked into the ivory eyes of Ella and stated, "This my dearest princess "Ella", is but my eyes, the original governor of the high seas, would you like to feed my dear friend some nuts?". He fetched some nuts from his pocket and passed it to 'Ella' who was visibly adoring the moment, she was now playing with the hiero-falcon and also stealing a glance towards the captain in a shy yet frivolous note. The falcon did enjoy this new company as an order for devotional harmony. He hooted a few times in honor and adored the shoulders of Princess Ella. The mini troupe, now broke into a melancholy chatter, as if they had been in a celestial bond of friendship, comradery and of course love.

The westerlies blew on, the sun was up now and candles were blown out, the waves danced to the tune of the majestic royal orchestra. The entire crew now broke into a frenzy of frolic and laughter, seamen broke into a dance, the legends and their beautiful partners enjoyed the sarcasm and seaborne dance moves of the seasoned seafarers. The effervescence of the scene resonated throughout the fleet. The captain ordered his mate to drop anchor until high noon the next day and he asked to relay the message to the entire fleet. He also called for a grand luncheon, followed by rest and relaxation until noon the next day.

The crew went visibly mad with joy at such a favorable yet unique declaration of order for the day by the majestic captain. Soon well smoked and barbecued turkey and salted tuna arrived at the grandiose dining table of the legends. Six portions were served along with fine red wine from the captain's private barrels reserved for an occasion such rare yet elegant.

The old head chef, the master of culinary arts stole a glance at the captain who was in a different world, another universe he was in, totally consumed and stuck in the expressive ivory eyes of Princess Ella. The MasterChef smiled and nodded in the irony of the situation and thought, "Good Lord, our beloved captain, he is but done for, bitten is he, by the notorious love bug, jeez look at him, he is possessed". With a bow he left the royal gathering and let the legends enjoy them company and food along with fine wine.

 The criminal excused himself and picked his glass of wine and finally strolled across the deck, on towards the stern, a rather quiet place now to adore the scene. Serene it was, blue waters, waves of melancholy, peaceful forbearing, one never felt before. A warm yet soft hand laid on his left shoulder startled he was, for the criminal of his demeanor or repertoire, none, no human has ever sneaked up to him, in such fashion without his knowledge before. He turned his head to find the evergreen eyes and young face, that of princess Elta, right behind him. A set of sparkling green eyes awaited unforeseen answers. She had followed him to find out his purpose for an excuse away from the royal muse.

Before he could even flicker or react, the sweetest voice penetrated his heart, mind, body, and soul through his ears of course. Lady Elta spoke in the purest of voices, "My Lord, the connoisseur from near lands, pardon me for prying with your thoughts, are you not happy with the proceedings for the day, does our company bore you, any reasons for your curious escape from a rather royal escapade, I pray if you feel I deserve to know the reason, please elaborate on the matter".

The criminal was astounded yet content at her probe. He felt a connection so dear and so true, which he had never weighed or experienced before. With the remaining confidence, he stated, " Dear princess Elta you don't have to seek any pardons for your probe and I am no noble, yes I am but a strategist to help out a divine cause of glory for our lands, but yet I am just a simple man, a commoner, without any royal forbearing; to be extremely honest, I love the current situation, the answer I know not why but I cherish these moments with you and that of the other princesses in your company and of course my dear legendary friends".

With a brief pause for fresh sea air he continued, "I have never been seaborne before or adored such beautiful sights, sights bearing tranquility and peace so dear and of course the company so pure, I feel I am swimming in this sea full of comfort and warmth, dear princess, I hope I have satisfied you with my answers, I pray".

Princess Elta looked mischievously at him and added with a flirtatious note, "I agree with your words of wisdom, but I still have a question, it Is something to do with what you just said, the part where you mention, you enjoyed the company of us three and your legendary friends of course, if I may tell me my lord of strategic forbearing, whom did you enjoy the most and find more interested or invested to know more off?".

The master criminal died for a moment, at such chivalrous words and could not hide his affection and interest, interest for knowing the unknown, infatuation incorporated thoughts which asked him, them thousandth questions of his feelings. That particular question though sliced him in two and he was red with the pressure of the blood, shyness engulfed him beyond doubt, his epiglottis allowed him to speak a few words.

Finally, he muttered, " Dear Elta, I have never felt this weird sensation before, one in my poor heart, but I feel I am falling for you, I don't know what it means but the intrigue and interest to know about you has grown in volumes, ever since I have set eyes upon you and heard your purest voice, Mi lady, please forgive me for such tame words, which just escaped my unleashed mouth, but I pray, the feeling is but real, kindly do let me know if the feeling is of mutual nature?".

The princess with pristine green eyes, now lowered her vision in divine satisfaction to portray her notion for eternal love and lean towards the criminal, finally, she whispered, "I think I have fallen for you too, dear criminal, you have but managed to steal my crude heart somehow, I concur I have similar feelings". With those words she kissed him on his cheeks and turned to leave, but was surprised to hear a soft thud behind her. Before she could react the majestic laughter of the two other couples interrupted her. Laughter that of the captain and the king along with their damsels in arms. Who were now but spying on with intrigue at the unfolding drama of romance near the stern of the ship.

Quizzically she looked back to find the criminal down on the deck with a smile. She laughed and helped in assisting the connoisseur of crime up on his feet. The criminal now in melancholy managed to mutter a few words of kindness, "You should not have done that mi lady I almost died, your beauty is too dangerous and your soul just blew me off my frail feet, I love you dear princess "Elta"".

With these words he kissed her in her sparkling forehead and held her in his arms, finally proceeding with a stroll towards the royal company, who was now in utter amusement and they favored the outcome of this short encounter.

The captain obliged to show the princesses their resting places, there was a mammoth cabin, right down the stern of the ship. It had already been prepared, ready it was with three beds. Princess Elta and Maria were exhausted and excused themselves to take a quick nap. The legendary trio scattered towards the main deck to catch hold of more frolic, ongoing in tandem. The king and the criminal had already joined the bosun, the first and the second mates on the main deck, dancing in merry they were. The legendary duo was welcomed with astounding cheers of joy.

The captain stopped midway to glance back, in order to inspect the atmosphere on the other ships in his fleet but was surprised to find the ivory eyed Ella right behind him. Her royal gaze almost blinded the captain, before he could get lost in the dusky mythical ivory of her eyes, the beautiful princess dragged him back to reality. She stated, "My Lord, O mighty captain, I see you are content at the proceedings of the day, you seem happy, which makes me even happier, I could not rest now, I feel I should let you know that we three sisters would like to give our heart mind and soul to this grand endeavor of you and your noble friends".

The captain smiled and patted her shoulder and finally added, " Dear princess Ella, you but worry too much, we shall conquer them high seas and the far lands, you and your sisters can rest awhile, rest you deserve and enjoy the grandiose moment". Ella looked uneasy at the high seas governor's statement and retorted, "My Lord, rest is for commoners we royals should endeavor for our hardship during majestic moments like this, this is the time for us to behold and enact, pardon my words dear captain, my sisters along with the legendary trio which includes you, is precious for me and my life to prosper, I shall protect it with my honor".

The captain was famished at such visionary yet heroic words uttered by the princess, he gave her a warm hug and the princess crept up to his seafaring salty cheeks and kissed it. Finally she turned and left to join her sisters. The captain froze to death in divine elation and creeping romance, one never felt before. The ex-Bosun, the now second mate crept up from behind, the entire plethora of hands, including that of the legendary duo on deck were closely looking at the captain in silence. The second mate whispered in his master's ears, "My Lord, I pray, let me know when I shall draw anchor off the ship, the one in which you are afloat, in your dreamland, of course, O guvnor, I see you have bitten badly".

The captain understood the sarcastic jibe of his old seafarer and in a funny note gave a short chase to grab hold of him, but the ex-bosun jumped overboard into the arms of the high seas, laughing out loud all along. The entire ship burst out laughing, the captain was caught red-faced in embarrassment again. The king and the criminal dragged him and handed him a bottle of his own private wine. The orchestra continued to play a romantic note.

The trio along with the entire crew went into a frenzy of dance moves flowing out of this melodramatic experience of valor and satisfaction of high sea affairs for the day. Able henchmen of the criminals did some insane somersaults to adore them royale legends. The frolic and funfair continued into the evening. The king was finally free at heart and dancing to the tune of the orchestra, a joyous note it was, a musical connotation of victory. When he finally caught the eyes of "Maria". The princess was looking at him with much appreciation and affection in her eyes. He awkwardly stopped his act of musical fantasy and strode towards the lady, who was now peering from starboard.

She was speechless when the king in a flash, like that of the westerlies, presented himself in front of her and smiled. He took a deep breath and added, " Dear princess, hope you and that of your sisters rested well, apologies for the noise, of course, today was great, but tomorrow I promise my dear, will be grandiose".

Prince Maria, one with them hazelnut eyes, smiled and instantaneously locked her arms around the king, finally kissing him on his lips passionately. His majesty had lost all his defenses, at that very moment and reacted gracefully to convey his righteous approach on this occasion. Lip locked were they for a while, finally, the princess retracted to breathe and found the criminal smiling in sarcastic harmony of the romantic undertaking and blushed, red she was.

She quickly bowed in front of the king and rushed to join her sisters, who were adoring the waves standing on the railings, towards the stern of the ship. The king quizzically looked back to find the criminal laughing at his antics. The connoisseur of strategy and crime hugged him, finally let out a few words sarcastically, "Eh, My Lord you have been bitten too, I suppose far and beyond, I believe".

The king retorted in a fake bravado, "Yeah you know my lad, I am but a fine connoisseur of romantics and that of love affairs, your commendation of me is but much appreciated". Both of them laughed at those words and in arms walked towards the captain who was now attempting a somersault. They caught him in the act and patted his back. Finally the criminal uttered, "Dear friend, my captain, no risks during peacetime, if I may, I pray, let us keep the princesses engaged, it's untoward if they are not briefed of the matters on hand".

The king declared, "My good captain, there are but other femme seafarers aboard our fleet, in other ships, of course, we have to maneuver our plans in such a manner that the three princesses are well taken care of and protected beyond doubt". The captain nodded in acknowledgment and led the way to have a few words with them beautiful trio, now adoring the view at the stern of the ship. Soon the fabled trio was there and the king broke the silence with the utter shock of the three femme fatale's. He glared, "My dear princesses, Ella, Maria and Elta, hope you have been enjoying the ship and its resources so far, I wanted to suggest that in such importance circumstances, like that of this, you shall board the spare, captured ships along with some of our able seafaring women fighters and finally set sail southwest towards that of our pure and dear near lands". He took a deep breath and added, "Worry not, you shall be treated as royals, as you were in your kindest of lands, my finest hand, "*the hand of the king*" is currently governing it with utmost diligence".

The three purest beauties known of them lands afar, exchanged glances and finally princess Maria declared with the confidence of the most divine kind, " Your majesty, my dearest king, I appreciate your concern for our safety but we are no feeble women, or "damsels in distress" as you may confuse us off, I accept your commandment but recommend that the two of my sisters, Ella and Elta take upon this seafaring journey on towards them near lands, as you suggested of course along with the entire contingent of female fighters at your disposal".

With a deep breath she continued, "But I, Maria, shall continue this grandiose journey towards the epitome of success for a common goal which we foresee, My Lord, I give you no option to reconsider my proposal, I believe this, my vision is just and of extreme importance for our future journey ahead".

The king and the two other legends were but taken aback at such pure message delivered at will by a human so dear, crystal it was with strategic imperative, glaring to comply and an uneasy thought of a seafaring princess associated with this journey. The king thought and thought but finally with tears in his eyes declared, "My dear Love Maria, you are but stronger than that of all seaborne humans on board, I know your zeal and commitment will never let you reconsider your judgement, hence I accept your proposal and therefore agree to the concourse of action for tomorrow".

He took a gulp of fine wine from the captain's bottle and continued, "The entire captured fleet of the far lands will be at your disposal, escorting our dearest princess Ella and Elta will be them femme fighters, I pray, both of you shall be helping our dear "*hand of the king*", with the royal affairs of the state and resting a royale' tranquil in the majestic royal chambers back in them dearest near lands, my ladies".

There was a brief silence in union and finally the old governor of the high seas, the hiero-falcon approached out of nowhere and landed on Ella's shoulders, in tears was it. The princess kissed it on its forehead and whispered, " O Kind governor, the eyes of them mighty high seas, please take care of the captain, he gets distracted too often, out of excitement, please direct him to the righteous path, farewell my dear friend". The king interrupted again in melodramatic fashion, "O Maria, as you mentioned, you shall join us for our endeavor, I the near lands king vow for your utmost safety and a forbearing".

The captain and the criminal resounded thy majesty's

commandment, " Dear Maria, princess, fear not we are at your service at all times, we shall but avenge our deserved pride by conquering them far lands, we promise".

The three sisters were in tears so were the legends. They hugged in accordance. The king hugged his favorite princess Maria, the captain, in turn, caressed his dear princess Ella, the eldest of the lot and the criminal hugged and cried on the shoulders of princess Elta, who was now consoling him dearly.

The MasterChef now broke their sad moment of emotional forbearing, he presented himself near them and stated, "Dear royals, the food is being served and with this great mood of valor and that of the day's victory I recommend we serve you the finest salted ham and port wine for an enchanting night to engulf us from within". With those words he bowed and left, equivocally the moon gods and them stars protruded and presented themselves in the vast night sky to govern.

The captain now heartbroken yet understanding the work at hand led the way for the final supper. "The Last Supper", he thought it would be, being negative was he, conservative in efforts. Finally the six of them sat at their designated seats in the grand dining table. They were served soon, with their portions and with grand port wine from the captain's seaborne cellars. The orchestra now played a somber tussle, one in sadness, a tragic note in musical tyranny, one to mellow out any human existence on board.

The entire crew was now eating and listening to the sad muse. Tears slowly rolled down their cheeks, and then they understood the proposition and the mood of proceedings to follow. With all the experienced of this seafaring years, they knew that their master, the governor was but not happy, and this pained them beyond their belief and that of their existence. The king stood and slowly trotted towards his quarters on the starboard side. He leaned on the railings and took a deep breath of fresh sea air. The captain looked at Ella, who was already deep in his eyes for answers. She took him by his hand and stood. She suggested him to follow and follow he did.

In a flash they entered the captain's cabin and a romantic escapade followed. Love and lust were but evident, during this emotional yet passionate encounter. Naked were they locked up in a cabin, infamous for valor but romance governed them beings today. Laughter and short chatter engulfed the vicinity along with heavy breathing, and the kissing continued. The criminal was but swift to steal princess Elta of her feet. He played with her and she played him with sarcastic yet frivolous intention, finally, they were in the criminal's bed, in an orgasmic orchestra never felt before. The king was disturbed in his melancholic experience of gazing down starboard watching the fish swim by. It was Princess Maria.

The night had set in, the moon god and them stars highlighted the swarm of fish below, to help in their nightly direction, on them high seas. The sharp edges of the moon, reflected brightly and sharp shreds of light fell on the princess, which made her glitter like a sapphire. Her worry ridden face was now evident to the king. He interrupted her sad thoughts and stated, "My Love, worry not, since the security that of your sisters, is but beyond secured. They would be safely harbored and well-taken care off ".

He took a deep breath one in an uneasy note and then declared, "But dear Maria, I worry for you, it's your proposition to volunteer for such a perilous escapade to unfold is but something somewhat unsettles me, I hope I can protect you with my life, I promise I shall do whatever it takes to fortify our progression and of course with the conformity of your safety at all times, Mi lady".

The now smiling Maria stated with her evergreen pride and astounding confidence, "Dear Majesty, my love for you is but equally proportional with that of my sisters, but your worry for me is absolutely not required, I pray, let me serve you, my Lord, I and my sisters are but well trained in martial arts of them far-far lands, we are equivalently well versed with swordplay and that of covert yet stealth borne attacks with precision for the definite success of execution".

She flirtatiously added, "Now my love, let me enjoy this day with you in a celestial union, intimacy is but the need of the hour, along with a romance of the highest kind, followed by a repose of course". She smiled and pulled the king by his hand towards the king's seaborne chambers. The king followed like a good shepherd, behind the princess. Once they were within the confines of the king's chambers, the voluptuous beauty held the king and started the act of heavenly romance. In a divine bond, they were, kissing, caressing, and riding each other in turn to keep the ignition of love aflame. Ravishing yet voracious love engulfed them, they were but locked in an inseparable bond of lustrous nature. Sweating they were finally, exhaustion engulfed them and they fell into a satisfactory repose. A sleep, destined for royals.

Similar was the tale in the other quarters which held the captain and his dear Ella, and that of the criminal and the princess Elta. In a grand repose, they were, resting at peace after a round of lustrous exercise. But destiny beckoned and soon they found themselves in reunion, in the fabled yet convoluted dream world. The trio had already observed this dream, partially before, but now they found themselves at the shores of them far lands. The easterly breeze again pushed them backwards and following their instincts they looked back to their utter surprise, to find them princesses. All three were present in the shores, to their utter astonishment, confounded they were in this vision from the future. They looked beyond them princesses, to find twelve ships of near lands origin.

Uncertainty and confusion engulfed them, but finally they embraced their better halves and progressed inland. Once again they found themselves in the midst of a vast bed of sunflower cultivation. They traversed across it to find the same hillock, which they had mounted before. They exchanged cautious glances at each other and drew out their mighty swords. With invigorating vigilance and utmost caution they progressed on. Whence they were atop the molehill, then out of the blue a few hooded assassins pounced upon them from all sides. Quick to react they were this time around and in the unity of valor and excellent swordsmanship displayed by all six of them. They in turn managed to overpower and slay all of them assassins.

Blood splattered everywhere, smiling at each other they were, with bloodied faces. The contentment of victory resounded in their expression. They soon continued their journey, now traversing through a limitless field of fine paddy. When they had reached the middle of it all, a poisoned dart flew out of thin air and struck the captain beneath the ear. The mighty governor of the high seas, fell down unconscious. Princess Ella rushed to check on him, with tears in her eyes. But before she could do anything, a peal of humongous laughter engulfed the monstrosity of the surrounding atmosphere.

A hooded assassin, with dark clothes, protruded in a distance, he lifted his hood to unmask his identity. It was a familiar face, but only for the captain and his seasoned seafarers. The far-lands merchant, the conniving one who had betrayed the captain's words, the traitor who had devised devastation of the captain's fleet on the previous occasion, even after the captain had awarded him freedom after defeat in them high seas. The crooked merchant who had pushed his noble friend unto the sea, the kind one who understood the captain's prophecy.

He now laughed at the royal gathering before him. But since the captain was now slain, so was his dream, rather cut in half and he woke up in a shock. The mighty captain was relieved to find his beloved Ella by his side. He took a deep breath, one of divine satisfaction and went out onto the deck to grab a pail of water. The dream, now rather a nightmare, continued on for the rest of them. Only the captain was unsure of the dreamy reality of it.

The far-lands crooked merchant now waved his hand in the air and dozen more assassins appeared. Encircling the legends and that of them princesses as well. A flurry of actions enforced and unfolded in their dream world and soon they all found themselves being dragged through the vast lands into a dingy cell of a dungeon. And similar faith construed, with a deafening sound of the loud clank of a padlock. Again they were reassured of their imprisonment in the far lands dusky dungeon.

In utter shock and animosity they woke up in a sudden jerk, back in realistic circumstances they were. The morning light was evident now through their sea-bound window panes, the Sun god shed a few light rays in the uncertainty of the situation. The criminal looked towards his beloved Elta, who was now but looking at him with an air of unsettled and shaken nature as if she had seen a ghost. He held her tightly. Similar was the fate in the king's chambers. He and Maria were in a tightly knitted bond, sweating were they.

The captain on deck now was maneuvering his ship and that of other ships in his fleet, in an excited fashion. The westerlies had gained pace and it was but evident, that the anchors were to be lifted sooner than expected. Princess Ella ran in from behind and held him dearly, the nightmare had affected her a lot, but the captain was unaware of the rest of the dreamy affair. He hugged her tightly. Finally he kissed her on her forehead and called upon his first mate. The captain's favorite seafarer now produced himself in front of his master.

He commanded his first mate to inform the king, the criminal and the two princesses of the deterioration of the weather, and that eminent action for preparation and departure of the two princesses was required immediately.

The first mate ran immediately to fulfill his master's commands. Soon the legendary duo flanked by their beautiful better halves were on the main deck. Awaiting were they for the captain's final commandment and course of intricate yet required action for the day. The entire crew judging the situation, gathered on deck in astute attention. The captain took a deep breath and glared out loud, " My dear friends and able seafarers, the westerlies have shown their true colors of the destructive kind, the weather from now on shall only but deteriorate further, I suggest that the lovely princesses Ella and Elta to board the neighboring ship which we conquered yesterday".

With confidence he further added, "All femme seafarers shall join you overboard and I command to equip all seven captured ships to be fit for the seafaring expedition back to them dearest lands, the pure and real near lands at the earliest". The first mate took a bow, so did the second mate and the Bosun, in union their entire crew retorted, "Ahoy, Ol captain, your order is our command, consider it done guvnor". In a flash they scattered to hustle for making their master's vision come true.

The hiero-falcon, swooped down from the skies and perched on top of princess Ella's shoulders. The captain smiled and nodded. He knew the bird's suggestion for the vigil of his dearest Ella and that of princess Elta. The intelligent being wanted to protect the captain's desires and that of his unfaltering vision.

The orchestra played a parting song, heart-rendering it was. Tears of uncertainty yet filled with divine conformities of love and love alone now gripped them royal couples on deck. "Au revoir" they glared in a union, the two of them sisters now bowed and left to prepare for their new homebound journey. The rain god cried in tandem and poured out his chest full of remorse on the fleet below.

--XXXXXXXXXXXXXX--

12. The Tragedy

"Life is but ironic to those who think and a tragedy to them who feel. Events in this world can be either good or bad, great or tragic. But when tragedy strikes, we are but miserable for the moment or sometimes even longer. It is but the way of life or the thought process of a human, to make the decision, of either observing and feeling tragic or to see it in ridicule by adoring a satirical lens".

The two princesses were now on board the captured ship, along with femme warriors and able sea hands of them near lands. All seven ships now ready for a seaborne voyage, back to the near lands shore, back to the safety of thy homeland. Farewell begun as the captain nodded for them ships to sail homebound, of course with sadness and a heavy heart. The rain gods cried profusely, therefore those tears of sadness of parting ways were but in-evident.

The legendary trio along with Princess Maria now waived them adieu. Soon the ships faded away trickle by trickle, out of their outlook into oblivion. The westerly's had a nasty smile on their face and which in turn had a ghastly effect on the fleet, with the gale-force becoming unbearable every passing juncture. The captain ordered his first mate to lift anchors and set course for them far lands. He relayed the same in a cursory manner to the rest of the fleet. Soon they were but sailing expeditiously, on towards their ultimate destination.

Lightning flashed everywhere, thunder followed in succession, dark clouds marred the morning sky and the horizon had the look of a gloomy evening. The high sea was extremely excited too, high tide and huge waves flourished, navigation became difficult in them troubled waters. But able hands they were, the captain's seasoned sailors. They maneuvered them ships with great zeal and that of gallantry. The captain led the legends and the princess to drier spaces, unto his cabin.

Four chairs were occupied swiftly, the chef's mate brought in hot soup for the occasion. The king was eager to discuss their future course of action. He took a sip of the fine soup, wiped his lips and declared with precision," My Lords, Mi lady, the weather gods have but stopped favoring us, as the mighty captain had predicted the westerly's to show their true colors, it of course seems that they did, I propose that we proceed with caution as visibility has deteriorated and the war in-land is still a distant proposition, least we need now is further surprises at sea".

The criminal smiled and nodded, finally he added," Dear Majesty, what an elegant yet immaculate insight for the fortification of the common goal you have, I admire your words, I agree my Lord, its caution I believe we must make sure off in these unsettled waters, I had also made sure one-half of our seaborne gains were loaded onto them ships bound for near lands, of course for safekeeping back home, the reason I choose not to send out the entire lot is, because on the contrary as of our seaborne course, them homebound ships are traversing against the ghastly westerly's, God forbid if anything untoward to happen, pardon my negative thoughts, I beg".

The captain took a deep breath and then stated," Excellent work my dear friend, thank you for your impeccable foresight and righteous action you took upon yourself to deliver, you are correct, our lot, them homebound, they are but up against them nasty westerly's, it's a difficult proposition and absolutely right for you to take such actions, the segregation of the wealth for further safety and protection, who knows what fate beholds down in them far lands for us".

The princess was but speechless until now, finally she spoke her heart and mind," You are definitely correct in your approach to strategize and to execute such a mammoth task with great vision and precision, I would like to highlight though, the fact that my sisters are but well versed of them naval and seaborne skills of navigation, cartography and that of high seas sailing expeditions, worry not as they are able enough to maneuver them ships in circumstances what nature holds for them, but for an imminent matter of maneuvering through these rough waters and hit them far lands with safety, precaution is a mandatory element, I suggest we use our best skills on deck to keep vigil and take heed of the information, which our dear hiero-falcon carries, I pray".

The king glared with passion," Wise words of brevity Mi lady, I concur, we shall abide by them". The trio nodded in union and so did the princess Maria. Finally the captain stood and stepped out onto the deck to relay the right set of instructions for the foreseeable future, which but held strategic importance.

The weather gods played on with a nasty note, the orchestra had found a dry place near the hold. It played a somber tune, a musical connotation of tragedy and sorrow. The bosun was all wet and in an unknown sorrow. He finally smiled when the captain forced himself on the main deck in this ghastly weather. It was as if a great messiah had pronounced himself and appeared for the commoner's satisfaction to preach them the righteous way forward. The captain struggled but ultimately reached up to the bosun and whispered in his ears for the impending course of action.

The mood and the air in the captain's quarters, his favorite cabin, was but that of melancholy and silence. Thinking and strategizing were they, for answers which had no ends or leads, ones which could relieve them of the pressure they felt. The master chef intervened their thoughts and it was but the mark of noon. High noon it was, but the weather gods concealed its identity. He and his mate accompanying him, laid out their luncheon of ham, bread, hot porridge and of course rum, old sea rum which the captain had stashed away for special occasions.

They thanked the chef and his mate and finally asked to inform the captain on deck to join in for supper. The captain joined them soon, his face sullen and filled with uneasy speculation. They nibbled on, least they ate was a morsel and then a morsel again, unhappy were they, consequences construed and played with their imagination. The criminal finally broke the uneasy lull and stated," I have a thought pressing my mind since them wee hours, Its but about a nightmare, rather a continuation of a day-mare observed previously, a quite peculiar one indeed...".

Before he could finish, three sets of cutlery fell on them plates with a large clank and the others were looking at him with ever-growing interest. The king interrupted his speech and retorted," Good lord, you saw it too?, even I did, we were all there in them far lands, is it that one where we get dragged on them far lands and finally lead and locked in a dungeon at the end, and of course the second time with similar consequences, except the captain is struck down and we have been joined by all them beautiful princesses?".

All three let out a consolidation of affirmation by uttering a unanimous "Yes" out loud, but the captain now intervened to query his short-lived nightmare. He questioned," Did you say struck down, was I?, all I can remember seeing was on the second time around, we were in that stretch of limitless sunflowers and all of a sudden the dream was abruptly cut off and I was awake?".

The king looked at the criminal and then towards Maria. Maria now finally spoke out to confirm," Yes dear captain, you were but smacked down in the dream and to be honest, I believe I saw only one dream, not two, Yes I am sure I saw "Ella" and "Elta" there too, surprising isn't it, I know not how this mysterious yet mythical episode had foreseen us and the very reason why we all saw it with such realistic proportions, is but quite intriguing".

The king nodded and looked at the criminal," Do you remember observing twelve ships, I bet I counted twelve, in each of them nightmarish dreams and of course, seeing princesses "Ella" and "Elta"; in them far lands shore was quite extraordinary too". The criminal looked at the captain and princess Maria and they all nodded in a bewildered admission of the vision.

Finally, he added with a grave face," Strange isn't it, Your highness, for us to see such dreams in union and with such trivia, especially when we are but just about raining conquest upon them lands, one thought though had affected me from the second dream, there was this mysterious hooded assassin, one who kick-started the second wave of attacks, I pray, I have never seen that face before, my lord, do any of you recognize him?". The king and the princess shook their heads.

The captain queried again," I have to assume, this happened but after I was mowed down, as you mention, I believe, I saw no unfamiliar faces on the contrary". They all took a sigh in disbelief and anxiety engulfed their noble minds. The captain stood and left to check upon the proceedings on deck.

 High noon it was but the sky and the weather were forlorn, the gale thicker now, rattling against the stern of the ship. The ships had gained speed, but visibility remained horrible ahead, they were but blind. The trio of the king, the criminal and Princess Maria, soon stood, bid farewell for the afternoon and left for their chambers at high sea. A mammoth struggle it was now, to traverse even a foot at length on the starboard side. Finally they all managed to reach their respective chambers.

Maria fell down on her bed and looked sideways, she felt remorse as well as a longing for her bubbly yet best friends in life, her dear sisters. Missing were they, empty were their beds, in melancholy and in a sudden sad vibe of separation, she shed a tear of regret. The mood of the desolation outside made her sulk further, soon she found herself in repose, rather a sudden afternoon nap waiting for her to embrace. And embrace she did.

The king was tired of looking out of the window. The criminal's words and that of them others had stirred his thoughts, he was intrigued by it all. He turned to look at his bed and then he smiled and reflected aloud," Good Lord, is that where the answers lie, them unanswered tales of the unknown". He rushed back to his bed and soon was in a divine slumber in a gloomy wet afternoon on them high seas.

The master of stealth & strategy was now in deep thoughts in his floating chambers of them high seas. Never did he have to brainstorm at this length to find answers, answers of ambiguity, answer's not under his control. Imagination played a cat and mouse game with him. His intuition was but unique than that of the others. He looked up and opened his windows, but them westerly's slammed it shut, before he could react. Frustrated was he. He stood and strolled around in his shaky and turbulent confinement atop them high seas. His ever searching eyes finally fell on his bed and the grandmaster of crime smiled. He jumped on top of his lofty bed, closed his eyes and dreamland beckoned in a flash.

Vivid dreams they saw. Forcing they were in a way to be in the exact spot, but dreamland denied them their request for long, playing with their imagination for fun. The trio rolled from one end to the other, as them high waves rocked their ship. The captain, his first mate, the ex-bosun now his second mate and the newly appointed bosun as well, were but maneuvering the mammoth ship with valor. Along with them able henchmen and his finest hands of course, but weather denied them a smooth passage. Even signaling other ships in his fleet was but impossible, visibility due to them dusky skies and the mad gale restricted their operational ability to stay in touch. The orchestra now found itself in the chef's quarters and they played a tune, now audible only to the master chef and that of his mate.

~ ~

Tragedy had struck in them seven ships bound for the near lands. The westerly's were against them and they were but without any fighting chance to salvage anything fruitful. Thrashed were they, all along by the nasty brute force of the gale. Most of the ships had lost their main mast, half-broken were they, barely surviving such a vicious blow at them high seas. Both the princesses "Ella" and "Elta" were manning their ship, along with other brave female seafarers. Destiny turned their hopes against them and then disappeared.

~ ~

An intricately curious affair now brewed on in the quiet shores of them far lands. The afternoon gale had harbored a soul, lying was he in them shallows, now almost unrecognizable. Naked was he, seaborne for long with the help of a log of wood, a buoy, a log of hope for long. Tiredness and fatigue of fighting them perilous waves, for a reason so divine yet unknown kept him going until he was but ashore. Finally his exhaustion capitulated his determination to stay awake and he too found himself in a dreamland. A dreamland too pure to ignore.

~ ~

An insane storm had brewed in them waters where the near lands mighty fleet now trotted. The captain's esteemed bird, the precious hiero- falcon now flew in, slightly injured it was. He dashed and fell next to the captain on deck. He bleated out eleven times in urgency and then unconsciousness engulfed its precious soul and it rested. The captain picked the great bird, patted it, hugged it with a warm embrace and rubbed it to bring it back to life. He shed a tear in sheer frustration and was devastated by this nasty course of the event.

A flying piece of broken mainmast hit him on the back of his head and he was in his subconscious self-bearing moment of an unknown yet tragic excursion. The first mate and the bosun saw their captain's state on deck, reacted in a flash and soon lifted him, along with his favorite bird. Finally bringing the inseparable duo back to the captain's personal cabin. The first mate was all in tears now, but the weather gods concealed his emotions by draining out them constant flurry of rain & dastardly winds of them madness bound westerly's.

Finally on his bed, the captain was. His most cherished pet laid in repose by his side. His best sailors closed the door to his cabin so that he could rest awhile. A blinding spear of lightning flashed. Them growls of the thunder gods followed. The ship was now almost tilted port-wards. And them king, princess Maria, the criminal and that of the captain and his pet rolled portside, fortunately still in bed, not spilling onto them hard Oakwood floors on the interior of their intricately designed chambers.

Dreamlands so common yet of so a tragic nature bestowed upon them. All four of them now found themselves in them far lands shores again. They looked back, the legendary trio, and the princess Maria too followed their act in intrigue. They counted twelve ships of them near lands again. They saw "Elta" and "Ella" waving near the shore in harmony. Finally they were together again. They strode on skeptically this time around, caution was the need of the hour. Soon they found themselves in front of the sunflower vegetation. The king looked at his legendary duo of friends, they nodded in unison. The criminal now led the way, trying to encircle the vast sunflower bed. Not traversing across it.

They kept on going the Far East of them sunflower engulfed lands, but the stretch was never-ending. From afar came a few assassins, hooded they were. A barrage of darts flew in and caught the captain, the king and them princesses. They were but pushed into a deep subconscious state and all they could see was the orchestra in them blue skies above, playing a death note. On their backs they were, battered down by them poisonous darts. The criminal was but in his senses, all darts had failed to get hold of his flirty body moves. Them assassins encircled him and that of the others. Finally a similar concourse of actions overtook and they were but all dragged to that same dingy dungeon of them far lands.

The criminal saw a hooded figure approaching the grills of that nasty dungeon. He took his hood off and smiled. The same face it was, observed in his last dream, the hooded assassin of them far lands. Smiling was that conniving bastard at him and at the rest of them noble souls, who were now down and out. The criminal looked deeply at his opponent, before a blow landed on his head and he saw sunflowers of the most divine nature. They slept on, all of them saw a sunscreen of sunflowers to relate in their subconscious. Finally one by one they awoke, understanding their futile efforts to unearth anything further in that dream was but fruitless and unequivocally unreasonable.

First the captain woke up and heard those urgent knocks on his cabin door. He opened it in a flash to find a worried face, that of the second mate, his ex-bosun. His favorite hiero-falcon was on his ex-bosun's shoulders. The mighty bird had earlier broken one of them panes of the captain's cabin and flew out to inspect the affairs on deck. Even though in semi injured state, he knew a guvnor-less ship, is but a ship of doom. And since the captain was injured and in slumber, he did not disturb the legend.

But now matters have gone from bad to worse. The red-eyed angry falcon struck the captain hard on his forehead, with his beak, out of frustration for not answering his beckons for battle stations or off caution. The captain bled from his forehead, where his favorite bird had struck. He came to his senses and glared out loud, "Battle stations, enemy ships ahead". His declaration was relayed all over, in an instance of flurry. Even the royals were up, swords drawn were they.

All henchmen jumped out in union to defend the near lands ship. The second mate whispered in the captain's ears. He declared that they had already lost four ships to them voracious weather gods and the tenacity of the westerly's, with all crew on board and that they were but thirteen ships afloat at this very moment.

The captain was aghast. The seafarer, the second mate now added on with further bad news. He mentioned that a mammoth fleet of eleven ships in formation of them far lands has but encircled them. He said that they are but fast approaching. Thirty meters for impact he said. The fable trio looked at each other and glared a war cry, "All men, prepare for impact, Ahoy, all hands on deck, let's murder them all".

Princess Maria jumped on to the main mast and climbed on like a spider to the top. She was positioned right next to the bosun. The poor fellow had a fright, surprised was he to see a young princess in such a ravenous mood. The captain raised his hand and silence prevailed. Swiftly the hiero-falcon flew out towards the port side to inspect. After a few brief moments of pin-drop silence, the falcon flew in low and crashed in on the main deck, next to the captain's wheel. Gasping for air it was, struck by an arrow on his wings. The captain lifted him, released the arrow, gave him a warm hug, tears falling with anger and as well as that of compassion.

The chef's mate took him off his hands and down the hold he went to the kitchen, to fix the old governor of them high seas. The mighty captain stood in agony, yet glared with passion, "All hands hard to port, prepare to engage, I want heads". With a burst of confidence and revenge burning in his bloodied eyes, he promptly turned them giant wheels and maneuvered the ship to hit side-on. Portside it was where the enemy approached.

Soon the ships clanked and ropes were flung from both sides. Assassins jumped on deck, captain's finest hands and that of the criminal's able henchmen fought them back. A grave encounter took center stage. The entire fleet was now under siege by that of those far lands fighter ships. Intense battle followed. In the main deck of the captain's ship. Two able yet noble hands succumbed to injuries and fell to their primal repose. The captain in anger slew a dozen, but them far lands assassins were cunning, they crept from in behind and slashed a blade on his back. Before the first trickle of seasoned seafaring blood fell on deck, in came flashing the infamous criminal and slit the assailant's throat.

The captain glanced back and smiled at his friend, the injury was but an exterior one. He ignored and continued his fight for supremacy. The king on the other hand had boarded them far land's ship, along with a few fine henchmen of the master criminal. They were on a strategic rampage to get closer to the hold, as well as that of the enemy captain who was found slaying another able seafarer. They swiftly butchered a few to get nearer, but the far lands captain's bodyguards were but valiant fighters. A gritty sword fight took center stage. A determined arrow, missed his majesty's heart but scraped his chest, and a few droplets of blood fell on the deck. He looked at the direction it originated and found the archer.

In a flash, princess Maria had but uprooted his head, with a flash of her sword and it now rolled on deck towards the stern of the ship. They smiled in a holy rapport and fought on. Thrusting closer towards the enemy captain, the king now tore a bodyguard apart with vengeance, into two distinct halves. Another hooded assassin stopped him in his progress but before his blade met and greeted his majesty's own, an arrow split his brains in two. The king now turned to find Maria his beloved, spraying arrows of vengeance at them guarding the enemy captain.

Bodies fell on deck in tandem and blood drained on towards the hold. The finest henchmen of the criminal, finished the improbable job with astute efficiency, throats were slit in quick succession, and soon the small troupe, one led by the mighty king had now encircled the bandit captain.

Fear and fatality, defeat and dejection, engulfed him and he finally dropped his blade and bent a knee in total surrender. The bosun glared out loud, "The far lands captain has surrendered, drop your weapons". The brave yet remaining fighters, who were engaged in the mighty captain's ship of the near lands and that of their own far lands vessel; now in shock looked back to confirm. The captain and the criminal found an opportunity beckoning and plunder followed. Heads of them far-land fighters scattered everywhere. Their moment of confusion had turned the tide of the grave battle. The princess now broke in through the encirclement and stood near the captured captain, with a sword on his neck, of course. The far-lands captain's jaw fell in utter shock and he wet his pants.

Maria, now with vengeance boiling, revenge reaching new heights, growled at him and stated, "You pathetic downtrodden thieving bastard, you who murdered my father in cold blood, you who mercilessly ordered for me and my sisters to be imprisoned in a dingy hold, you who stole every possible belonging and gain's we had, I am here to put your gluttonous and thieving soul to rest in hell, of course". With ever-growing anger she glared, "I promise you, I shall help my dear majesty that of thy near lands, to make sure every filthy mongrel, every undeserving far land scoundrels shall be but beheaded to honor our vision for greatness and security from scum like you". With those words she spat on the now shivering enemy captain and beheaded him with a powerful strike of her mighty blade.

The head fell on deck, Maria kicked it hard and it flew out of the port side onto them high seas. The criminal and the captain's first mate now broke into the hold to inspect and secure what was but deservedly theirs. Huge explosions in them high seas stole the essence of victory and all victorious souls of thy captain's ship now laid their eyes on the devastation across their fleet and that of the remaining far land's ship.

Ten far lands ships, excluding the one they were upon, were but on fire. Along with that two of their own were set ablaze. The fighting of the high seas infamous clash had been one of a kind. There were but casualties on both sides. The far-lands conniving assassins had set ablaze two of the captain's finest ships, even though they had lost control of their entire fleet. Moreover, they had booby-trapped each hold to explode if captured. There were but no gains in this seaborne war. Most of the captain's able hands who had overpowered them far lands ships were but blown into smithereens or burnt in the process.

Malaise prevailed the evening as the infamous trio now sat on the main deck. All but dejected at the colossal loss. Princess Maria was a bit contented that she had the opportunity to slay the conniving enemy captain. The evening had turned into night. The captain's old first mate now produced himself in front of them royals. He was soon joined by the second mate. Crestfallen were they, heads bowed in shame. The captain stood and hugged them, knowing their condition. He finally asked them, "Dear lads, you did well today, this is but war and there is always casualty in war, my friends, tell me give me a detailed account of our losses and gains".

The first mate looked at the ex-bosun, who with teary eyes beckoned in a faltering tone," Master, "sob...sob", we have lost two of our ships, them crazy assassins of the far lands were but on a suicide mission, they slaughtered some of our fine men, we fought back bravely but their holds were all but booby-trapped with firewood and a mechanism to ignite them explosives, we lost all gold and them gold". With a deep breath, he continued, "Moreover, we have lost two f our magnificent ships with all men on board, we are now but left with eleven good ships, all half-filled but with fine hands to see us through my lord".

The king rose and patted the ex-bosun and the sobbing first mate. Finally, he declared, "My men, we have won this fierce battle, one I have in my short stint as a ruler have never embraced or stumbled upon, I am proud of you all, kindly relay the same to all hands on deck of this marvelous fleet of my dear friend, let us advance tomorrow, towards them thieving far lands and restore justice and deal with their resistance for good".

The criminal and the first mate was fortunate not to open the hold of the captured ship earlier, due to them timely explosions. They were but saved since even the conquered ship was also but sabotaged to blow out loud. The captain ordered to set the ship ablaze, and it was fulfilled in an instant. He further ordered the first and the second mate to set sail on towards them far lands.

The king went down to his chambers to rest, so did the criminal and followed by the princess. The captain went down to the crooks quarters to check on his beloved bird. The hiero-falcon was but awake now, he had regained strength, thanks to the cook's mate for the timely bandage which healed it beyond imagination. Actively it flew and landed on its master's shoulders, the captain patted him and held him in a warm hug and cried. The falcon shed a tear too, understanding his master's loss immediately. The captain took him up to his finest cabin and put him to bed and he himself dropped his anchor and went into a divine repose.

A few days went by, them eleven ships hovered over them high seas without further action or adventure. The westerly's have had enough too, and now but retreated for the moon year.

~ ~

The far-lands noble merchant had now but opened his eyes. He was in a hut, near them shores, as he could hear them waves and smell of dried fish. A lady in her middle ages entered the hut and greeted him with warmth in her eyes. She finally explained that she had but found him. Lying naked on them shores. She further stated that she had but no one to care for, hence thought it would be apt to harbor him for a few days until of course he was but strong enough to move about. He thanked her dearly but tiredness had engulfed him and soon he melt down into a heavenly repose.

~ ~

The wind was still now, awaiting for the easterly's to break the silence. The sky was bright, just them souls afloat were in a mood of gloom, the fabled trio was on deck with princess Maria, when suddenly the bosun cried out loud, " Landmass ahead, we have made it, Oh god, there is one of our captured ships ahead, one of them seven which was en-route to our glorified lands".

There was a sense of urgency on deck now, seaborne souls hustling to get a view ahead. The captain jumped atop the mainmast, next to the bosun and took out his field-glass to inspect. After a while he looked down and quizzically nodded towards the princess. Princess Maria joined him at the helm of the mainmast, took the field-glass to probe and finally let out a sigh of relief.

"Tragedy is but an illusion, a feeling short-lived if treated with a daring vision for the primal greatness of achievement".

--XXXXXXXXXXXXXXX--

13. The Incarceration

"Confinement can be self-imposed, in that of the walls of one's mind. Imprisonment can be of domestic nature too, but incarceration is generally associated with forceful abduction and finally confinement or imprisonment for starters. The angel now had a look so tragic in his face, yet gathering his stature he continued further....."

The two ships now clanked with harmony, a few ripples of faith formed astern. The lead ship that of the captain's own, and the captured ship yet the one which was homebound; the one which bore them princesses Elta and Ella were now in friendly conjunction with that of the captain's vessel.

The Green-eyed princess and the beautiful ivory eyed demi-goddess now looked on. With tears in their eyes, yet with content to finally see their sister Maria again, and of course their beloved captain and the criminal. There were only fourteen femme seafarers afloat on that ship. Rest had lost their lives, fighting for survival in them treacherous weather conditions created by the westerlies.

They came overboard in torn clothing, which portrayed the devastation of the weather gods. Once on deck they were embraced by the awaiting royals, with warmth and satisfaction they craved for, all them passing days spent apart. The entire crew hailed them, femme sailors, for their daring adventure and fighting spirit in terms of battling for survival in such great fashion.

Maria led her sisters to their chambers, washed and clothed them. Finally all six of them settled in the mahogany table. Princess Elta informed the captain of the tragic loss at them high seas, due to uncontrollable circumstances, but declared that they managed to grab hold of a drowning ship before it was too late. She and her sisters along with the help of their brave female crew had managed to gather all gold and gains into their own hold. But with remorse she added that all six other ships were but lost with everyone on board, in the arms of the angry high seas.

The captain opened up his heart to them, with an unfettered mind. Brimming with an experience invigorating and tears of happiness in his eyes he added, "Mi ladies, you have but made me proud beyond belief, none, no human had ever triumphed at the feat to fight against them westerlies and stay alive to tell the tale, losses in these seas are a common affair, but survival is a story even greater". The king now confidently glared, "I am but proud of you ladies, I concur the captain's vision for the greater good, now we should plan and strategize for the conquest in-land, one which shall mark the completeness of our mission and bring conformity to our souls". The criminal nodded in union and so did Princess Maria.

The pristine blue waters below were but still. The Sun gods awaited for governance of peace below, but faith had a different plan in mind. Maria stated with divine confidence and an air of conservative realization of the future course of action. With a heave of breath, she glared, " My lords, your majesty, my dear sisters, the most favorable thing for now to proceed, would be to traverse in-land, but without the entire crew, that is the eighty-four men on board and them fourteen lady warriors; I suggest that the four of us, me, you my lord, your majesty, the captain and of course the criminal bestow upon this journey to examine the landscape at length before compromising or engaging our seasoned forces on this conquest".

The legendary trio saw reasoning and wisdom in Maria's proposition. They nodded in conformity, but her two sisters retorted with understandable resentment at the decision. Them three, they argued at length. Finally the king had to intervene to make them realize the gravity of the loss at this stage and of course of the actions to foresee, for their hardship filled days ahead. He glared in confidence, a declaration utmost required, "Dear princesses, we shall go inland but only four of us, as princess Maria had mentioned we cannot but lose heads or blood of the most sacred kind, which belongs to our kingdom, I order all of thy near lands ships to raise anchor and honorably retract to a spot in these high seas where they can see the shoreline and wait for the orders from the admiralty".

The criminal added with divine gravity brewing in his heart, "I agree your majesty, we should not disclose the number of ships, or of our headcount, without clearly understanding the scale of war this could lead to, in these lands, it would be apt if the ships were far from the shoreline, but at an optimal distance where the captain can see them with the help of his field-glass and signal them to enter center stage, whenever opportunity prescribes".

The mighty hiero-falcon now fully recovered, flew and sat on the captain's shoulders. He smiled at it and suggested, "Of course if we foresee bad weather or any situation which calls for any urgent signal or messages to be delivered, we have our good friend here". All of them smiled in unison and nodded in appreciation and corroboration at the prowess of the great bird. Soon the mini troupe was near the helm of the ship. The bosun was lowering a small boat, unto them shallow waters of the shoreline, fit for the four of them.

The captain was found arguing with the first and the second mate. Both courageous and seasoned seafarers were now, showing their disagreement on the decision that only four royal's would form the initial expeditionary party to scout the landscape. But the decision had been made, that the two princesses and them two able seafarers would command the assorted near lands fleet, until further notice for the primal conquest. Finally they agreed and the entire fleet lifted anchor. Once all four of them were down on the boat, Princess Maria looked up and waved at Ella and Elta. Both seemed to be worried, but waved back and shouted out, "Good luck and Godspeed".

The entire fleet disappeared swiftly and by the time the scouting party was dragging their boat ashore, the fleet had completely disappeared from the horizon. The captain looked back and pulled out his field-glass to inspect. His jaws dropped in horror. Maria, the king and the criminal looked quizzically back towards them sparkling waters of the shoreline. Two heads emerged, that of Ella and Elta a few feet from them. A naughty smile materialized on their faces, the other four heads now shook in dismay.

Maria added in excitement, "I knew it, it's just impossible to keep you two out of any action, isn't it?, come now join along". The hiero-falcon now flew and sat on the captain's shoulder. The captain asked it to relay the message back to the first mate that all of them have reached the shoreline safely. He also told to convey that the princesses, Ella and Elta had also joined them, hence the fleet will be under the command of the first and the second mate, until further notice. The great bird hooted once in affirmation and flew back towards the horizon, where the fleet was last seen.

The criminal and the king had by now hidden the boat in a bush. Well concealed it was, out of reach of any prying eyes. The mini troupe' of three damsels, armed to the teeth and that of the fabled trio now commenced upon their scouting expedition to map the landscape of them infamous far lands. Trotting across the sparkling white sandy beach of the foreign land were they. Soon they entered a coconut grove which was but placed intricately at the end of the shoreline. The captain threw out his cutlass and six fine juicy coconuts fell with a thud. They enjoyed the fine pristine yet natural glory of the coconut water as they traversed in-country.

They now saw a demarcation, which was well devised to keep them high waves flooding the mainland, a small hillock it was. Soon they managed to get on top of it. The scene below was marvelous yet bone-chilling. It was a never-ending stretch of sunflower cultivation. One which they had seen, in them recurring dreams at the high seas. With shock written all over their faces they looked at each other. The criminal broke the silence and muttered, " Twelve ships, them princesses Ella and Elta joining us, the sunflower belt, never-ending as it is, that pathway lining it, the only thing missing so far I bet is them devious assassins and of course the presence of the easterlies.

The easterlies responded instantaneously at his words and blew a mild gale which pushed them back a little. They smiled, yet uncertainty and the effects of the wicked dream engulfed their mind, body and soul. The prodigal son of the nature gods. The infamous sun god, now highlighted the pathway below, in a way to suggest caution and consequences hidden in it.

The mini troupe was about stepping downhill towards them pathways when they heard a loud scream behind them. They turned to find a female, definitely a far lander, waving towards them in a cautionary note, from within the coconut canopy. Her words were but blurred, due to the noisy easterlies now gaining momentum. But before they could walk towards her or react, a group of hooded assassins appeared out of thin air and encircled them.

The legends and the three princesses formed a close-knit circle and drew out their swords. The princesses had two each in their hands, them legends one each. The easterlies blew their hair sideways, but their vision was unfaltering. Soon the assassins made their first move of engagement and came forward to strike home. In a flash there were hooded heads splattered across the demarcation, like assorted meat for a grandiose luncheon. The legends had barely managed three kills by now. But the valiant princesses had slaughtered them entire lot, without even a sound of impact, of them blades kissing one another.

The entire vicinity was but bloodied and bloodied were their faces too. They glanced at each other, smiling in eternal perception and with the satisfaction of victory. The criminal looked towards the canopy behind, but could not find the pious lady who tried to caution the party before. The others too tried their luck in finding her in them coconut grove, but failed. The criminal now turned towards the sunflower vegetation and fell into a deep thought.

Finally, he uttered in an imaginative concourse of a statement, " The easterlies are but evident, the first wave of the assassins are dealt with, it happened rather sooner than expected, the mysterious noble female who cautioned us, is but of divine intrigue, but what lies next is grave and requires extreme caution".

With a deep breath and chest full of them chilly easterlies he further added, " My concern is but not able to make out who that hooded figure was, in them dreams, the one who slew the captain with a poison dart once before, and last time round he even got all of you to perish, in that nightmare, and then he engages in an act to let out his real identity, I pray my friends, I have never seen that soul before in my life, have you? I know not why, but dear captain, he has a special dislike for you my dear friend".

The captain and the criminal were eyes locked, in a convoluted harmony for a while. Finally, the captain with a deep sigh retorted, "Interesting, isn't it? that every time my dream was but short-lived, and as you say, it might be the case, wherein one of my old enemies of them high seas, has but conspired with us all, pardon me my friend but no familiar faces or names, one who can construct such a villainous effort to challenge us, mighty souls, has but ever crossed my mind".

The mini troupe now looked at each other for answers and someone to lead the way. The criminal broke the reticence of uncertainty and added, "We have had taken the longer path down them sunflower bed before, also avoided it the last time around and taken the pathway towards the east of where we stand, with similar consequences in our dreamy escapade, I suggest we try them westbound pathway this time around and embrace reality as it unfolds".

The troupe now nodded in union and in conformity of the proposed course of action. Down they went unto them pathway, encircling the limitless sunflower beds, then progressed on westwards. Swords drawn, in a state of utmost caution, were they.

An eerie breeze and then finally a cloud of dust followed in from behind, they turned to inspect. Soon a flurry of poisoned darts rained, but all of them were taken down by a brilliant display of swordplay. One reeking in the finest of martial arts, by them femme goddesses. A dozen hooded assassins appeared out of the dusty clouds. Mounted on horseback were they. Soon they encircled the mini troupe. An assassin dismounted and took a few steps forward, distinguishing himself from the group of assassins by wearing a red hooded cloak, in contrary to portray his leadership.

Before he could react, princess Maria glared out loud, "You filthy coward, low lying Cossack of the highest kind, if you have the least of dignity or valor to fight us, identify yourself before we behead you and observe your presence diffuse from the face of these lands, with the help of the pace of the easterly winds of course".

The criminal smiled at such probing jibe at the assassins ring leader. The effects of them words, of the beautiful princess, pierced the pale yet feeble heart of the assassin. He immediately took off his hood to reveal his identity. His blood was boiling with terror. Finally, he glared out loud, " You naïve near lands tramp, you dare to call me coward, I am but a famous far land merchant, one who dealt with gold and that of other gains, until this man, the conniving captain of yours, usurped my gold and threaten my existence".

The captain now laughed out loud and declared, " O God almighty, thank you, my lord, for sending such an easy bait, to protect and represent the first wave of resistance', you faggot, you whom I gave freedom, now try to deceive and stop me, I shall behead you for sure".

A gritty battle took center stage. The three princesses quickly decapitated an assassin each. The criminal slaughtered one but two other guerrillas attacked him from both ends. One slashed at his left hand, wounded him and he fell off balance due to its impact. The two assassins, now closed in on him to finish the job. But the king cut one in half and pierced the other right through the temple.

The dead assassin fell down with his head split in two, the criminal nodded at the king to convey his vote of thanks. The captain had slain four cowled assassins by then, with his prowess and finally he approached his primal prey, that of the larcenous far lands merchant.

Two bodyguards blocked his way and he had to engage with them before reaching that rapacious merchant. One by one he defeated and exterminated them. He was about to turn towards the thieving merchant, when the conniving ring leader, taking advantage of his unawareness, thrusted his blade, which now got lodged in the side of the captain's chest.

The fraudulent merchant retracted his blade and prepared for a final blow to finish the mighty captain once and for all, but then, something out of them blues upturned the situation. Out came flying, the mighty old guvnor of them high seas and tore off his arms, holding the blade in a flash, with his vicious beak. Fear consumed the two remaining assassins and that of the bleeding merchant. They instantly boarded three horses and fled the scene.

Ella was devastated to see the captain wounded and rushed to tend to him, with tears in her eyes. The king and the criminal rushed and mounted two horses, they looked at the captain and nodded. The captain responded with valor and nodded in return. An acknowledgement of the fact that he was all right and that the duo should follow in pursuit of the thieving bastard before it was but too late.

The captain stood, ripped open his cloak and his vest off. Finally he went near a dry patch of weed growth, picked two stones and instantly lit a small fire by striking them stones against each other. He welded his blade in it trying to make it hot enough. He took out a bottle of rum, off his cloak, drained a quarter of it unto his wound. There was no reaction of agony or bitterness. He smiled on and asked princess Maria to follow them legends in hot pursuit. Off she went in a flash, leaving a cloud of dust behind, atop a fine dark gazelle.

Princess Ella tore some medicinal weed, smashed and rolled it, finally squashing it into a paste. Finally the blade was hot the captain placed it on his raw wound and instantly it was but closed. He emptied the remaining rum in his dry throat to balance out the consequences of his feelings. No pain no remorse, left his straight forward reaction to the pain inflicted. Soon he let Princess Ella apply the medicinal paste upon it as a disinfectant finally he wrapped it with a torn piece of cloth off his vest and stood. Ready was he, the war machine, for further concourse of the historically important moment unfolding, quarter by quarter.

Princess Elta closed in towards that of her sister Ella and whispered in her ears. She left in flash towards them coconut groves, mounted on a spare horse. Soon she was but gone, disappeared into thin air and dense vegetation. The captain quizzically looked at Ella but she let out a blink of an eye, to restore the captain's hopes and resound the fact that it was but necessary. The falcon, the great bird was but nowhere to be seen.

Them love birds, now in solace, the captain and that of his dear princess Ella finally mounted the only spare horse. They left together in a blaze leaving a puff of dust behind and progressed on towards them raiding party. With the hope of retribution and grand conquest, they rode on eagerly to embrace destiny. The sun gods couldn't hide his excitement and blew out all his rays of light at once, and soon it was but a day so sunny.

Them easterlies paused and looked back at the drama in-land. The king was throttling at full speed on his finest horse of them far lands origin. The beast was worried about disappointing his majesty and hence gave his heart out, in a fashion which it had never done before. The king was but a furlong behind them assassins and that of the thieving merchant. Not far along, followed the connoisseur of crime now brimming with eternal determination.

The hunters and them being hunted now entered a parched pathway. More civilized it was them surroundings. People peering out at the majestic yet grandiose of events unfolding in and near the town center, in the artistic decomposition of greatness never observed before. They finally embarked upon the capital city, their horses now pleading for mercy. Soon a large dark mask formed the horizon before them. A few meters forward they went on and found that it was but the entire far lands army. Awaiting their arrival on the pilfering merchant's intricate yet larcenous message. A message full of betrayal to capture the king and his fellow royal's.

A plethora of drugged darts flew across and hit the king. He hit the ground soon, falling off his horse. One of them darts hit the mighty criminal too and he went in an instant repose. The gathered crowd jeered and hailed their king who was but waiting at ease along with his army of hooded assassins. Laughter and chatter followed. Finally the cunning king glared, " My fine merchant, you have done a great job at nabbing them bastards, look at these mongrels my dear citizens look, their fate could have been yours, but no! They choose their fate! So rejoice and make me happy, now praise me and disperse immediately that will be all".

The guerrillas dragged the king and criminal through the city streets unceremoniously. Enforced cheers, hailed the conniving king and his deeds. Finally the duo was led to a dingy cell, in the far lands dungeon and locked up for good. Sleeping were they, in the harmony of the unknown yet known sequence of consequences forbearing.

The citizens glared out one last time in fake harmony, "Long live thy king of far lands", before leaving back to their rather faithful quarters. Unhappy were they, but happy was their ruler. Filthy was their living but frivolous was his character and his fake governance. He and his conniving ministers now laughed out loud and retracted towards the grand courtyard of the high castle. Princess Maria saw this horrid affair from afar. Intelligent was she, not blinded by anger to pursue an unforsaken task. But gathering Intel and confidence to accomplish the unthinkable. She dismounted from the horse near a barn, of them far lands and vanished into its arms.

In a few moments time the captain and that of his dearest princess, arrived at the same scene unthawed. A few prison guards and that of the remaining assassins saw their approach and let out a few more poisoned darts. They too fell down in a drowsy repose. Similar actions construed and they were but dragged unto the same cell. The padlock clanked to confirm their imprisonment.

~ ~

A guard now ran towards them grandiose royal chambers, where a feast of the most magnificent nature was but unfolding. He ran towards the conniving ears of the far lands king and whispered. The king was but busy fucking a gypsy whore, hence pushed him back. He glared his red eyes at that of the loyal messenger for disturbing him.

Finally regaining his senses, at the gravity of the news, he stated, "Dear nobles, we have but captured that bastard, that dark yet conniving mongrel who has taken almost all our gains; one who threatens governance of a sovereign kind, one who talks of peace and tranquility, that poor captain, is but in our hands finally, his prophecy won't last a day, I declare let us behead all of them at high noon tomorrow". The entire plethora of assassins and thieving nobles of them far lands glared, " As you wish my lord, your order is but just, hail thy king, behead them, filthy souls".

The cunning merchant leaned towards the far lands king and kissed him in his cheeks. Finally he muttered, now in a drunken stupor, "I have but lost my arm, due to that nasty bird of his, I shall behead him myself, oh king! Kindly grant me that honor". The crooked king looked at him and nodded in acknowledgment. The dastardly orchestra played a tune of thrifty nature, it was but the representation of the far land and of its torrid reality.

Booze fell on them floors of the grand courtyard, drowned in wine were them all. Naked dancers pried onto survive them rapist's eyes. Some were but devoured in front of the afternoon skies. The sun gods, but had enough. The torture and them rape grew as if animals reigned their city; but this was them far lands, where the law was but outlawed. Where peace was at war.

Finally the sun god retired and let the moon gods bestow his heavenly direction. His celestial presence and his heavenly undertaking were but extremely necessary that very day. He governed them late evening skies in a bold fashion, along with them stars for a reason. The easterlies quietly obeyed too. The population in turn prayed for the gods to intervene.

--XXXXXXXXXXXXXXX--

14. The Conquest

"At times war is but inevitable. The two utmost authoritative avengers of war are patience and time. Sometimes it is well planned, on certain occasions it just strikes you off-guard and you react. But one thing is certain; in war, the legends always outnumber them foot soldiers ten to one". The man in white nodded in a celestial understanding of the narrator's thoughts and listened on keenly.

The easterly's sounded disturbed and now blew out its gale in an uncanny, haphazard manner. Princess Elta had finally crossed the coconut plantation and now was in the stretch of white sandy beach. Instincts told her to progress on towards the right, that is but towards the west of them far lands. She slowly trotted across the sea of sand. After a while her prying eyes, caught upon a trail of footsteps. She pursued it with an invigorating passion to know the unknown.

A few seagulls hovered over her in a quizzical manner to inspect the proceedings below. Elta progressed on with an air of urgency now. Soon she came upon a thick foliage of open shrub. She circled around it but lost them tracks of the unknown savior. There was an opening within the thicket of shrub and she took the path. When she had but reached the middle of the thicket, the unknown lady, the mysterious one, now presented herself from within the foliage.

She was unarmed, but Elta out of caution and recent misgivings, left no stones unturned to uplift her best practices of primal vigilance. The mysterious lady was but of her middle ages, fair-skinned yet looked to resemble a fisher-woman of them far lands.

She raised her hands in an honorable surrender, "I presume you are one of them near landers? Me and my friend, the survivor we saw your ships; are you going to save us from tyranny? Are you? Anyways why don't you follow me, you need to meet my friend. He has but some important propositions and words of caution for you!"

Elta was but taken aback. Before she could react or probe, the mysterious woman started walking down towards a pebbled path. She followed her at a distance, keeping a keen eye on them surroundings for any last moment surprises in store. The lady now pointed to a small hut in close proximity, near another patch of open shrubs. Finally they were on the doorstep of the hut and the middle-aged lady knocked on them doors, in a musical rap.

The door opened and a tired-looking man appeared and smiled. The lady asked the princess to follow them in. With a heart, mind and soul filled with uncertainty yet trusting her divine instincts, princess Elta entered the house. A house of a commoner it was, one she or her sisters had never explored or adored before.

The hut was small but apt, well kept it was. The tired man, in his middle ages now sat back on his bed. He had dark circles carved in them honest eyes. Smiling was he, politely. The mysterious lady, not that mysterious anymore due to circumstances and occasions, finally smiled.

With a deep breath of homely air she spoke, "Dear near lander, hope you are here but to liberate us all as I mentioned before. My friend the merchant has more to enlighten you off, than me, but I would like to welcome you to our lands without any malice in our poor hearts". She nodded and smiled, so did the noble merchant.

Princess Elta nodded in harmony but before she could speak, the lady brought her some fresh coconut water and served it, as a gesture of homecoming. Elta gracefully accepted it, took a sip and declared, " My dear lady, good merchant, yes I am but a part of the near lands troupe, you saw us sail down here, we have certain aspirations and plans to set things right here, in them far lands, of course, first of all, I would like to thank you, my lady, for the timely caution, before them assassins pounced upon us earlier today, and moreover I would like to know how you knew who we were and our intentions? I pray if you may begin to explain and connect the dots of uncertainty for me".

The far lands noble merchant smiled and spoke for the first time, " Welcome near lander, I am but a far land merchant, trading my goods with goodwill and passion; a few moon weeks ago, we had a ferocious encounter at sea and had faced a mighty yet infamous near lands captain in them high seas, the loot in our hold was unfortunately not ours, but of them petty far-off lands, and a pious captain let me and another conniving merchant live, he granted us freedom, along with a boat to flee, too kind was he in such circumstances".

He coughed out loud and took a sip of water allotted for him and gathered his strength. Ultimately he spoke again," You see, when we were but half our way back here, my conniving mate argued and fought with me, he wanted to avenge them usurped loot and of course greedy was he beyond doubt at that moment, a far land fighter ship entered our horizon and he, out of them blues pushed me unto the treacherous waters; I was lucky a log fell off our boat, I clanged to it for life and then the gods took care of the rest, somehow this kind lady over here found me".

The easterly's penetrated them feeble doors of the hut and played with Elta's hair. She was eager to know more hence, she maintained silence and patience, allowing the gravely tired noble merchant to gather himself for further revelations. The exhausted merchant took another sip of freshwater.

He now spoke with rejuvenated valor," You know Mi Lady, that conniving merchant went ahead and joined them pirate ships of our wicked king, they must have challenged that noble captain again in them waters of the high seas, I was praying I see him again, I owe my life to him for saving me when I woke up today and saw them near lands ships in the shoreline, I gained my energy back to an optimal level, I then saw six of your folks in the white sandy beach, one of them was but him, "By Jove" it was but him!!, the mighty captain!; yet unfortunately, before I could shout out, this pious lady came back from her daily market visit and warned me that they were but already aware of your presence, in them royal square, and them thugs were planning on sending a sequence of raiders to finish you all, especially the instructions from the wicked king was to exterminate the mighty captain".

The saintly lady looked at young and beautiful Elta for answers and direction. Elta was finally at peace and she let out a divine smile after a long time. Satisfied was she with what she had unearthed. She finally added," My dear noble merchant, you have but enlightened me beyond my feeble doubts, I thank you a lot as you have helped the noble cause with your intricate observations and devout thoughts, I also thank you, dear lady, you had but warned us at the righteous moment, before them assassins attacked us".

She took a gulp of fine coconut water to quench her thirst and continued," We but butchered them assassins, but the mighty captain was wounded in the process, no need to worry as he is fine and them gladiators have but all left to pursue that thieving merchant you had mentioned off, he was there too in the assault against us, he had one of his arm chopped off by our devoted friend, by that of the captains favorite bird, I know naught how to repay you for such a generous act, but one day I shall".

The so-far silent spectator, the middle-aged kind-hearted woman, now finally spoke out," Dear near lands beautiful damsel, I adore your brevity and your courage, I wish we, the far lands females were but just as bold as you are, you need not thank us, we hate our ruler and his governance, we but want change and change of the righteous kind, I thank you for showing us the right way forward in terms of retribution".

The noble merchant added with growing urgency," Mi lady, did you but say, them friends of yours had left in pursuit of that larcenous mongrel, that bloody usurper?". Lady Elta nodded in cognizance. The merchant now turned pale at the acknowledgement. He finally stated," It's good that he is injured, and who in this sailing world doesn't know about the Ol' guvnor of them high seas, the precious bird must have but done enough, but I am still skeptical and worried, because if they but went further northeast of here, as my dear lady friend had described, the road but leads to the town square, where but hordes of guerrillas, of the crooked king of these lands, are standing guard to pounce upon any near lander".

Elta's face lost color. The easterly's also accepted and presented her mood. They had influenced them, weather gods, to let out an unexpected afternoon shower. Gloomy was the atmosphere, forbearing to keep it sad with a continuous downpour, ongoing until nightfall.

~ ~

Trickle by trickle the drizzle increased to an outpour. Maria understood the evident cover provided by the rain gods better than her sisters. She but let her horse graze in the royal granary of thy king of them conniving lands. Out she went adoring a cloak, she found in the granary, which belonged to one of them assassins, one who was but protecting the granary. The one she thought was but a necessary sacrifice in the war of all wars.

Her horse was but left tied in the granary for future excursions. She drew her hood down, when she embarked upon the pebbled streets of them far lands. She strode straight on towards the town square where a few guards stood on guard, to prevent any unknown person traversing into the walled city. Maria checked her pockets and found a pair of gloves, generally worn by them assassins.

In a flash she wore them and she but now looked exactly like one of them trained assassins, of the order of them far lands. On she went down the road, two guards looked at her and ignored her, as if she was but one of their own. She was delighted, her first test was successfully achieved, without an eyebrow raised. On she went, now in the middle of the beautiful yet dead, immoral city center. She looked around and saw the king's high castle, a tad afar was them wicked dungeon right next to the moat leading to it.

Maria inspected the shops. A market it was, where soldiers and assassins were but snatching goods for free. Them citizens paying by their sweat and promises for food. Soon her eyes fell on a saloon by the tavern. Off she went into it with a smile. She knew, the best place to gather information is but at a saloon full of Ol' drunken souls, cause a drunkard never lies.

She pushed them feeble doors open and found a table in the utmost important yet intricate place, right by the window on the far side. A few habitual drunkards hobbled around, blabbering an unknown rhyme. A customary sign of their harmonious existence reflected profoundly. A butler came up to her and served her a mug full of pale ale. There was no doubt in the butler's mind about Maria not being a well-bred assassin.

She smiled in her concealed yet stealthy look, one of honor. She took a sip out of it and almost squeaked at the bitter yet rather pathetic taste of the local ale. Calmly she looked around to observe and to hear what was but relevant for the greater cause.

Two elderly men in the nearby table, were now sipping their flash of golden bliss. Ultimately one of them rested his mug and muttered in a drunken stupor," Ye know mate, that bloody king of ours, has but nabbed the near lands majesty and two other males, ye... Also, they say 2 beautiful damsels, seems they were but about to relieve us of our misery, but destiny beckoned". The two elderly men now laughed at the rustic yet realistic joke and clanked their mugs.

~ ~

Stark blue were them skies, the orchestra played on in an adventurous tune. The first mate sat on the deck with a bottle of old sea rum. Awaiting any signs of the bosun, sitting at the helm of the ship to signal, of any news or signs of them expeditionary party bound in-land. The second mate was firmly perched atop the mainmast, adoring them far lands shoreline with his Field-glass.

Zooming in on a dark flying object, he now inspected it closely for its origin. Soon the tiny object turned into the great guvnor of them high seas. The hiero-falcon was but traversing at premium speed, tearing through them easterly's to deliver the utmost important message.

The second mate jumped down on board the main deck and relayed the message of the Ol' Guvnor's arrival. Flashing came the great guvnor, but this time around, it didn't land on the main deck. Instead the mighty hiero- falcon traversed swiftly towards the starboard side and rapped with his beak on the captain's cabin, and then on the king's seaborne chambers, finally trotting towards the criminal's quarters, he rapped on each door as he crossed them.

The second mate and all of them crew observed the bird's behavior with intrigue but dared not interrupt the Ol' Guvnor. Ultimately the guvnor stood in front of the princess's grand chamber, raised one wing towards them doors and turned his head, looking at the second mate. The second mate looked at the first and both nodded in acknowledgement. He ran to follow the guvnor's order.

Soon the second mate opened them doors to the princess's quarters. The mighty hiero-falcon now flew in and sat on princess "Ella's" bed. The captain's able seafarer nodded in acknowledgement and glared," Ahoy, Ol Guvnor, I pray, I understand you mean the four of them, that is but our beloved Captain, The almighty king, the master criminal and the beautiful princess "Ella", I concur, but my lord, what of them?".

The falcon flew and sat on his shoulder, he pointed towards the main deck. The second mate obeyed the falcon's command and in a flash they were there atop the center of the main deck. The mighty bird now jumped down and with his tenacious sharp beak carved out a big circle. He ultimately stood in the middle of the circle and looked at the second mate, then at the first.

Both of their jaws dropped in sheer horror. The second mate now engulfed with fear, glared aloud," Almighty Lord, Good Ol Captain, the king, our majesty, the criminal and princess Ella has been captured by them thieves".

The so-far silent first mate questioned the bird," But what of the rest of em'? Where are our dear princesses Maria and Elta?". The Ol Guvnor now jumped out of the vicious circle and uttered a large squeak.

The entire fleet let out a large sigh of relief, knowing that they were but safe. The bosun looked at the two able sailors and enquired," What now Sire? how do we free our lords and murder em' thieving little monkeys?" The first mate whispered in the ears of his second in command.

~ ~

A rat strolled happily with utmost freedom across the untidy floors of the cell. It finally found the tired king's uneaten piece of bread and nibbled on it. The king was but exasperated of banging on them caged doors of the cell; with no answers to his arrogations. Princess Ella was sitting on the side of the mighty captain, who was but sick and tired of kicking on them walls of their dark and dingy confinement in the grave dungeon of them far lands. The criminal was but unaltered by the entire episode, sitting at one corner, thinking deeply of the possibilities of escape and that of retribution.

Dark was the cell, built with large boulders and painted with ash. Dejected were they and deprived of honor they deserved. A few moments later the dungeons main heavy doors opened with an enormous screeching noise and footsteps could be heard. Them footsteps grew louder. Finally the conniving merchant stood in front of the prison doors, looking at the royal prisoners and smiling. He broke into laughter, his hand now covered with a bandage, to cover the Ol' Guvnor's exploits.

With loathing pride he glared, "Oh look at you poor filthy near landers! How is the service dear majesty and you bloody captain? Hope you are enjoying the kind hospitality, ha ha ha ha ha ha, let me tell you that the plan is but set, we shall behead you four by high noon tomorrow, to mark the beginning of our far lands feast, one celebrated in honor of our mighty king".

With a sneer of sarcasm he finally added, "Of course, when he is but triumphant in battle or had won at war, but this time around, victory has been served easily, the foolish prey has but gifted himself without a fight". The thieving merchant's cold laughter echoed throughout the dingy cold dungeon. The king's eye's glowed in anger and so that of Princess Ella.

The captain jumped out of his sitting position and in a flash grabbed the rods of the cell door. He glared in anger, "You pilfering mongrel, you unfortunate brainless nitwit, my pet has just devoured your hand, I shall cut into tiny pieces of meat and feed you to them sharks, how dare you threaten me or my compatriots here". The conniving merchant turned to leave, waving a hand in sarcasm and mockery on his way out.

The mammoth doors of the dungeon were soon slammed shut. An Eerie silence of doom presided. Music of frolic in the high castle penetrated through the only opening in their cell, preparations for the grand feast had but begun. Bright rays of light entered through the windows but were lost in transition in the dark vicinity of the cell

All four now sat in a circle now around a spot of light on the floor which them prison window allowed them to adore. A small shadow appeared in their circle of light. Soon it formed a shape and before they could react to it, it took the shape of the Ol guvnor of them high seas. With a raised wing in honor of thy majesty, the king and that of the captain. With a startled mind and that of their rattled senses, all four of them looked upward towards the window.

The hiero-falcon was there, with a set of smiling eyes, an unique art in tandem. He had a scroll tied to his left leg and the intelligent bird pointed to it with his wings. The captain rushed to it, the window was far from his reach. He jumped and jumped but unreachable was the Ol guvnor.

The mighty falcon now understanding his master's plight, tore them threads, protecting the scroll and finally picked it with his beak and dropped it into the dingy cage. All four of them formed a circle of congregation, as the captain picked the scroll and read it. He ran and flicked off some of the thick ash of them walls. Finally he started writing a message on the back of the scroll, in the clear but unused side.

He looked up at the Ol guvnor of the high seas, then smiled and nodded. He crumpled the scroll, made it into a ball and tossed it upwards towards the Ol guvnor. The infamous bird caught it mid-air with his beak. The mighty hiero- falcon nodded in acknowledgment and flew out in a flash. Gone with the wind was he, instantly.

~ ~

The moon sky was bright, the dark flapping winds were but dictating them easterly's to behave. The Ol guvnor was on the prowl, of course bearing a message. A message of utmost importance. But he had other grandiose affairs of retribution in his mind. Ones that required immediate disposition.

He looked below in search of Princess Maria near the town square. He saw a hooded figure exiting the local saloon. Soon a thick layer of smoke evolved around the building, followed by a large bang. The majestic bird hooted in happiness, it knew that the act had to be the masterstroke of dear princess Maria.

Soon he swooped down to land on the princess's shoulders. She patted him and released the scroll which the mighty bird held in its majestic beak. One half of the far-land's army was now focused on extinguishing the blaze in their town square. Of course one which the clever princess had successfully executed.

She had struck a piece of firewood alight, and left it to burn near the barrels containing moonshine, which was but highly combustible. Now the fire had spread across half of the town square and most of the shops of the far lands flea market were up in flames.

The other half of the army was but busy organizing the feast, which would continue until the high noon, the very next day. It was to mark the successful capture of them near lands royals. She thought through on the probable course of action ahead, post-reading the urgent scroll.

Moreover, she did agree on the captain's direction for the approval of the criminal's master sleuths to sneak inland at night to free the royals. A brilliant idea bloomed in her mind and she took out her handkerchief, finally writing on it vigorously with a piece of firewood.

Ultimately she tied all them scrolls to the Ol Guvnor's legs and patted the majestic bird. The Ol Guvnor hooted and left for good from the town square to deliver the important message with sheer speed.

~ ~

A thick yet powerful brew of them seaweed and medicinal herbs had but made the far lands noble merchant better and fit for his most cherished escapade. He knew it was but his moment to repay the kind captain for his pious deed. The middle-aged lady, Princess Elta and the merchant now slowly trotted on horseback, to find traces of the captain and the others.

The Ol guvnor was relieved when he spotted them souls, from high above. He swooped in to deliver them the expedient yet important messages for better judgment and clarity for their future course of action. Soon he was but adoring the firm shoulders of beautiful Elta. The princess read all of them scrolls and looked up to the merchant with intrigue written all over her face.

Finally, she took a deep breath of the fresh yet thick easterly's and declared, "Dear merchant, our good captain, along with my sister, the mighty king and the master criminal, has been captured by the vile king of these lands, they now rest in a dingy dungeon near the high castle, the captain has ordered the finest henchmen of thy criminal to sneak inland during the night, but I fear their efforts will be diminished if not focused righteously on the plan of escape and retribution".

She let a sigh of relief and added on, " Interestingly my dear sister

Maria has but escaped capture, without the notice of them bandits and now has set ablaze to half of the town square, hence one-half of the vile king's men are now focused on damage control and the other half is but busy preparing the grand feast, one which is scheduled to begin tonight, and will continue until high noon tomorrow; when as per your conniving merchant friend, all four noble souls are to be exterminated to mark the end of the near land's existence, I pray, do you know of any probable route or plan of action, wherein the master sleuths of thy criminal can sneak in and save our nobles ?".

The merchant smiled and nodded. Finally he took out a piece of firewood and requested Elta to pass the handkerchief. He turned it and wrote his directive on the unused side and handed it over to the princess. She read it and smiled. Ultimately she tied all the scrolls back on the leg of the Ol guvnor.

With a large hoot in honor of the intricate proceedings, the hiero-falcon now left the scene. It soared high on towards them shoreline to deliver the primal message for the eminent course of action for the day.

~ ~

The Sun gods had but retired and the easterlies blew in tandem. The evening had set in. The moon gods appeared along with his friends, them stars. To watch closely, on the interesting course of action and developments below. This time around the plot was thick.

The first mate had but silently navigated and now had maneuvered his ship, in the cover of the dusky skies. The entire enemy fleet was near the far lands pier. All of the sailors had but left for the day, on the command of their vile king. Of course to the high castle, to enjoy the fest. A festival to mark victory without proper war.

A masterstroke they thought, their mad king had delivered. But destiny favored the brave, and reality was but about to turn its tide on them. Swiftly a few sailors, able hands of the master captain, now swam across to capture those unoccupied ships. Soon they had unanchored all them twenty ships of them far land's fleet. With utmost silence and caution they maneuvered them out into the high seas.

The bosun now atop one of the captured ships waved a lamp to signal the first mate. The first mate smiled and signaled back in acknowledgement. The near lands fleet had grown by three folds in a masterstroke of brilliance. The master seafarer, the first mate now, counted thirty-one ships, which were now under their command. The largest fleet to ever adore them high seas.

~ ~

An equivocally magnanimous atmosphere adored the nightly affairs in and around the town square. The far-lands orchestra could be heard from the castle by the moat. Tearing into the night sky it was.

Equally devouring was the pitch of the commotion of them assassins turned firefighters now trying to put out the ravenous fire in the town square.

In this multitude of commotion, the master criminal's finest henchmen had slaughtered them guards of the royal garrison, sneaked in and were now in hooded attire, similar to that of the far lands royal guards. They had learned the tricks of the trade by now, in terms of explosives and mechanisms to explode barrels of firewood by timing it to their advantage.

They had gathered all firewood and hay in the garrison and devised it to blow at the right occasion; as and when they deemed fit for the cause. A few of the henchmen had but used the cover of the night and their concealed outlook to their advantage. Ultimately they appeared at the doorstep of the royal granary, with barrels of firewood in their hands.

They entered and bowed to the congregation seated in harmony and with an air of divine gravity of satisfaction, that of the nightly affairs. Thanks to the Ol Guvnor's agile yet intricately delivered messages, the princesses Maria and Elta were now together. Seated were they in the granary, along with the noble merchant and the middle-aged far lands fisherwoman.

The Ol guvnor, the mighty hiero-falcon was on the contrary, rather busy nibbling through all possible samples of grains in the granary. It didn't even let out a morsel of worry or interest in the events unfolding. For it knew, the seeds of destruction and epic conquest of them far lands were but sown now, deep in the vicinity of the lands. War was but inevitable now.

A divine vision had he, but the operational undertaking, was but an important piece of the directive, one which laid on them beautiful yet hard shoulders of Princess Maria. Maria was in deep thought, when them master sleuths had arrived. She nodded at them in appreciation. But fell into her imaginary world of "if's and buts and them maybes", in a convolution of a strategic pathfinding mission she was.

The noble merchant had earlier enlightened her off the firewood in the garrison and the placement of the granary. He now broke the silence with an inquisitive intrigue to know more of her thought process and the royal directive of the imminent course of actions to foresee a well awaited victorious outcome. One which relived them far landers from their daily tyranny and the restoration of goodwill, along with trust amongst the populace.

He stated with a note of intrigue in his voice, " Dear princess Maria, you look worried, kindly let us know, help me help you, Mi lady, we have to but enact before the day breaks and of course there is but them royals, the king and the captain along with two others in the filthy dungeons, I pray".

Princess Elta's pristine green eyes now sought answers from her dearest sister. Distraught was she, separation from her newly found love, that of the master criminal, was but unbearable. Finally, Maria looked up and declared, " Apologies, I had to think this through, we need to divide and conquer this time, I hereby command, this stash of firewood to be evenly segregated, one half to be placed here in the granary, and the other half to be planted in below the only route to the high castle and out, the wooden bridge over the moat, make sure we time this to perfection since all three explosions have to be in sync, one in the garrison, the other in the granary and finally the only passage to be blown out, one which connects that conniving king and his men to the mainland."

With valor she further continued, " The reason we need to blow up the granary and the garrison, is but to cut down any possible supply of armament and that of necessities to the high castle, and blowing up the bridge absolutely converts the castle into a prison of its own, lack of supplies will draw them morons to surrender without a fight eventually; and of course dear merchant, this commotion of epic vandalism shall give you appropriate cover to rain down upon the guards in the dungeons, to finally free our noble souls".

The noble merchant nodded and left. The hiero-falcon was alert now, he sensed the course of action and flew out of the granary at once; destination unknown. Elta followed in behind the merchant to help out in the just cause. The granary was now mechanized to blow up on the righteous command of Maria.

The second mate left with a couple of fine henchmen to booby trap the bridge over the moat. Princess Maria and the middle-aged woman now left the granary and waited in the cover of darkness for the right signal to appear. The plot was getting thicker, impatience trouble her, but she managed. Maria was sweating over her plan, hoping and praying that all but went smoothly as devised.

Out of them starry skies in came the mighty Ol guvnor. It finally settled on Maria's shoulders and hooted once, his eyes glittered. The princess smiled and looked towards one of the henchmen, who was religiously awaiting her command. She nodded at him and the fine henchmen smiled and ran back towards the granary.

~ ~

The mammoth explosions tore out into the night sky. The smoke and the flying debris now marked the moonlight and the starry plate of oblivion above. The goddesses of ivory bestowed its charm for the eventuality of the forbearing proceedings for the night. There was a sudden silence and then havoc engulfed the atmosphere.

Only two guards remained now. Standing in vigil, in front of them dungeon gates. The rest of the guards had left to investigate the curious affair brooding in and around the town center. Confused were they, never had they ever noticed or observed such a treacherous yet convoluted event in their kingdom's history.

Two shadowy figures now produced themselves in front of them. The guards tried to defend and initiated a futile effort to investigate their identity. But even before their thoughts passed their mind and their hands reached their swords, they were but slaughtered mercilessly.

The hooded figures now inspected them fallen bodies closely. One of them stooped down to pick the set of keys, which would eventually open them mammoth doors to the dungeon. They had managed to penetrate the treacherous dungeon of thy far lands. They traversed across in search of their prize. Ultimately they were in front of the dingy cell, which but held them royals.

The king, the captain, that of Ella and the criminal now stood in attention. The captain took a few steps towards the cellar door to inspect. One of the hooded figures now opened the gates. He took a few steps into the dimly lit cage, bent a knee and lifted his hood to identify his presence.

The captain was glad to see the face of the noble far lands merchant. He helped him up and hugged him dearly. The merchant stated in absolute harmony, "Now my captain I can die in peace, as I have repaid your deeds in equal proportions, my lord, thy governor of them high seas".

Princess Elta rushed and hugged her sister Ella, then finally embraced her love, the master connoisseur of crime dearly. The mini troupe was but in divine harmony as they exited the treacherous dungeon.

~ ~

A large sound that of a trumpet resounded at the end of the town square facing the high castle. A hooded messenger stood atop a cluster of barrels. Them far land citizens along with the remaining guards now slowly strolled across, towards the figure to find the reasoning for his alarm.

Finally when the attendance was but satisfactory beyond doubt, the figure removed the hood. It was but Princess Maria. Brimming with confidence was she, adoring the mighty old governor on her shoulder. With a splash of determination and astounding courage, she glared out into the night sky and beyond, " I Maria, hereby declare war on these lands, surrender yourselves or be executed without a pinch of mercy, Amen".

---XXXXXXXXXXXXXX---

15. The Triumph and the Return

"Destiny prefers drama, hence, "Au' Revoir" is but an optimal option, but for humans, realistic yet achievable and favorable outcomes matter. Therefore, any human sane enough, under circumstances of importance prefers the usage of, "Ta' L'eme' Sy'ntoma", which in Greek, the language of the Gods, means: "See You Soon".

Them easterly's had mellowed down, autumn had but sunk in. The moderate climate and that of melancholic weather construed. A week had passed since them plethora of explosions shook the far lands to its core. A favorable 'modus operandi' had but besieged upon them lands. Them assassins, the royal guards and that of the ever eager yet thriving citizens had but surrendered their faith, their goodwill, finally acknowledging the just yet divine governance of the near land's ruler.

The far-lands had been conquered without much bloodshed, yet the denizens, the royal tenants of the high castle by the moat had been adamant. Surrender for them was but taboo, disbelief engulfed them. Lack of food supplies and that of armament, constricted their zeal to fight and defend longer. Squeezed were they, without a decision on their favor. Caged in their own prophecy of doom, imprisoned by their fate and their unjust deeds. But hunger and thoughts of death surpassed their futile resistance. Ultimately a white flag protruded from above the gates of the high castle.

A truce was sought. Irony and cheers followed on, from them observers beyond the moat. The king was having his high tea, with his friends and acquaintances in the town center. The town center was but restored back to its original state and it resembled a happy market place with a courtyard to entertain them near lands royals.

A secret adversary, a fine henchman of the master criminal now approached the mighty king and spoke in his ears. The king smiled and nodded. He stood, so did the other royals. Soon they were near the moat. Victory beckoned and conquest completed. They embraced each other in harmony at the sight of the flag. Finally the captain ordered his able hands to draw them mammoth siege ladders unto the castle walls.

The criminal appeared in royal attire and whispered to the king. The king nodded and glared out loud," All fine henchmen of thy master criminal to oversee this siege of the high castle, the master shall guide us on this journey, proceed with caution, trust none of them thugs confined up there". He looked at the criminal and added," My friend, all of us, the captain and the princesses will but follow your command on this intricate yet necessary affair".

The master sleuth took a bow and lead the line of attack on to the high castle. Soon the raiding party was atop them high walls of the castle. The criminal was looking at the devastation below. Most of them far-lands assassins were but dead. Hunger and fatigue had but taken its toll on them. A few zombie like creatures now, out of sheer hunger, were but nibbling on some of them fallen souls. Cannibalism was provident. A rotten smell, a mixture of shit, piss and dead meat now filled the air. The vultures hovered above, some devouring the grandiose mass meals down below in the royal courtyard.

The captain saw a familiar figure and in a flash jumped below. He withdrew his sword and closed in on his primal prey. Yes it was but the one-armed, conniving merchant of the far lands. Eating rotten human flesh, was he, of his own countrymen. Fate and destiny had shat on his thieving soul. He was but weakened in his mind, body and soul.

He looked up sheepishly and terror overwhelmed his physical existence beyond imagination. He shivered in fear at them bloodied eyes fixed down upon him, them revengeful eyes of the mighty captain; whom he had but double-crossed. The entire troupe now walked on and joined the captain. The master sleuth's, that of the criminal's own, now finished them weaklings in a flash. A couple of them broke open them doors to the king's chambers, in order to capture the thieving majesty of thy far lands.

The captain smiled at his enemy. The fallen opponent now, with a trembling hand tried to plead. But the Ol' Guvnor, now swooped in and tore off one of his eyes. The great falcon now sat on the cunning merchants' head and nibbled on the remaining eye. The blind yet cowardly merchant now cried out in sheer pain, but all his efforts went in vain.

A masterstroke of thy heavy sword of the captain, a seasoned piece of flint, which has but seen many opponents perish, now pounced upon the enemy. In a flash the thieving merchant's head rolled on in the courtyard. Vultures followed it with ever-growing eager to replenish their hunger.

The troupe hailed the captain for slaying the downtrodden mongrel. An enemy so great yet was no match for them legends and their faith. Triumph was about to settle in when one of the henchmen of the criminal broke the harmony and produced himself in front of the legends in a hurry.

He stated in urgency," My lord, O mighty captain, Your honor, I have some very bad news for you, apologies governor, the thieving king has but escaped the castle, we found a tunnel dug out from the chambers, running down below the moat, out into them stables south of here".

Them royals were but taken aback by the news. The king ordered for a search party to investigate and comprehend the fleeing far lands mad king. To break the utter confusion, the criminal who was but silently weighing up the pros and cons, finally uttered. "Dear friends, I feel it's but too late to capture the conniving king, tell me, captain, had the sailors of yours, anchored all them ships and travelled in-country to rest and enjoy the triumph?"

The captain nodded and stated," Yes dear friend, all my men had laid anchor to our enhanced fleet, near the shoreline where we had disembarked, and since we had but conquered these lands, without much fuss of course, I had ordered the men off duty to rejoice and cherish this moment in-land, tired souls they were, relief and confidence was but necessary you know, is there any problems you foresee, O lord of strategy?".

In deep thought and with intrigue brewing heavy, the master criminal added on, " Mmm, I suspect on something fishy, I pray, your majesty, let the search party first inspect whether all them ships of our fleet, is but intact, cause sea is the only route which seems feasible for an escape from death for the thieving king, the in-land cover is always a bad option, since the entire far lands population but craves for your just governance my lord; anyone who sees him shall report of his whereabouts instantly, I smell a rotten fish here my lord".

The king nodded at the criminal and then at the captain in acknowledgement. The captain in turn ordered one of them, henchman, to immediately set out a search party along with his first and second mate to find out about them ships.

The easterlies blew on, the Sun god bestowed enough light into the matter in utter intrigue. The noble citizens had volunteered to clean up the messy courtyard and the royal escapade of the high castle. Soon it was but established back to its original state; the castle sparkled in love and passion. The king, the captain, them princesses adored the royal chambers with their presence.

The far lands finest musicians played on along with the near lands finest orchestra. A grandiose note in harmony it was. Triumph of them lands was but equivocally evident. Citizens happily paraded them streets, singing songs of victory and praising them legends and of course them beautiful princesses too.

The restoration of the town center was but almost complete, with the help of the captain's able hands and that of the finest artisans of them far lands. The scene was set for a grand festival, one which the far lands had never observed before. One truly great, to mark happiness and the beginning of them conjoined dreams of glory days to besiege.

A tired seafarer now entered the royal chambers. The royals looked upon him with intrigue. He walked up to the captain and whispered in his ears. The almighty captain's happy face turned grim. He dismissed his fellow sailor politely and looked at the king with urgency.

Finally gaining confidence he added," My Lord, Dear Majesty, forgive me, I was but foolish, the master criminal, our dear friend was right to suspect foul play, one of our ships of the near lands fleet, has been stolen, we are but left with thirty ships now; the point is that the thieving king of these far lands has but managed to escape our prowling eyes, God knows where he shall traverse to?".

The king thought awhile, but finally declared," My dear captain, worry not, we have but won these lands, our might is but restored, we are victorious, small misgivings happen everywhere; what can such a small, tiny and exclusively filthy ruler, with not many men under his command do to great legends like us and that of our magnanimous army?, I pray, let us enjoy this day, tomorrow we shall start the voyage back towards our homeland, moreover I have a few announcements to make".

The criminal entered the royal chambers along with the noble merchant of them far lands. In deep thought were they. Finally joining them royal's thy master of strategy added, "Your majesty, as the search party has found out, the thieving far lands mad king has fled, I pray, there is but only two options he has, either traverse towards our own near lands or on towards them far-far lands, I worry his political influence can gain him popularity for avenging us in the future".

The king smiled and waved a hand for his friend to sit. He finally declared, " Dear friend, you worry too much, I love you for taking up this weight off me, just like our friend the captain, I pray, let us but enjoy the day and traverse to our homeland, which dearly awaits our return".

Princess Maria looked at her sisters and smiled. She stood and added, " Oh come on you legends, its time for fun and frolic, the merry, all tired souls need, a victory not celebrated is but half-cooked, kindly enjoy this day, let the episode of entertainment and greatness begin, cheers".

She raised the toast of them fine far lands wine and the royals joined her in the great gesture. Soon all of them were in smiles. They strolled out in the royal courtyard where thy orchestra boomed on in celestial harmony. A few naked belly dancers now displayed their curvy moves. Divine was their muse and that of the mood. Denizens and that of the citizens sang, drank and rejoiced this great moment. The grand feast followed. The entire population was invited to enjoy this very day in the magnanimous royal courtyard of the far-lands.

The Sun gods beamed their happy rays to mark the celebratory moment, citizens danced and sang aloud, songs of praise and harmony of them lands. Wine poured on, music flowed like them waters of the high seas.

A couple of excited courtesans dragged the second mate and the bosun into one of the royal chambers. The captain was laughing at the scenes. Soon them gypsy escorts, invaded their privacy, once they were but locked up with the bosun and that of the able seafarer. A voluptuous episode of sexual fantasy engrossed the confined proximity. Never had those seasoned sailors enjoyed such erotic moments of celestial bliss. Cries of lust boomed out of the close proximity, sweat and tears of joy covered their faces.

A mild gale blew on in them courtyard, the king looked at Maria and smiled, she smiled back. The captain was in a detailed debate with his beloved Ella, a conversation of the most ironic kind. Laughter and passionate kisses bestowed. The criminal was brooding in his thoughts, with a glass of fine wine, in the toe end of the courtyard. He was flanked by the noble merchant of them far lands. As usual thriving for answers unknown.

All of a sudden the king stood and with gravity lurking in his voice, he declared, " My men as I had stated earlier, we shall proceed forward with our plan to traverse homebound tomorrow at first light, I hereby declare the master criminal, as the governor of them far lands, but since destiny beckons, he must travel with us to the near lands, for now, I suggest the noble far lands merchant, be thy "hand of the king", one to oversee the affairs of the state of these fine lands".

With a gulp of fresh air, he rhetorically added, "My citizens, worry not victory is but ours for long, I promise you these short misgivings shall not stop the progressive nature of our lives going ahead, before I start boring you with a lengthy speech of stately governance let us but cherish this moment of greatness, let's make merry when we can, that would be all".

The entire plethora of attendance glared in a union, " Long Live Thy King, a king so just, the messiah of the epitome of success of the near lands and that of the far lands, we hail you, supreme leader, may we all prosper in your heavenly governance, Amen".

The fun and frolic went on, unto the night. The moon gods danced in celestial harmony, played hide and seek with them clouds. Them stars blinked in a naughty note. Happiness, lust and celebrations of the highest kind continued. Victory rang in every corners of the lands. The easterly's traded their resounding story of triumph afar.

~ ~

In the following peaceful morning, the legendary trio along with their princesses were on board the captain's ship. They looked upon the humongous gathering formed ashore, in the shoreline of the far-lands to bid them safe passage. The "hand of the king", the noble merchant was but waving along with the middle-aged woman, at them royals. The royals devotedly responded back in harmony. A deep reflection of solitude followed, them citizens cried in tranquil, in sadness, cause of the parting messiahs of freedom.

"Au revoir", they screamed and waved goodbye, awaiting their king and guvnor, the mighty criminal's return, when the time was but ripe. The royal orchestra now settled on the main deck and played on a parting song. A melancholic note in appreciation and musical grandeur. The easterly's had retreated for the moon year to party with his old friend, that of them westerly's. The sun god, bestowed his heavenly justice of light to hail the parting yet victorious souls. The high seas maintained decorum to ascertain a safe yet undramatic passage for the near lands fleet of them thirty ships to traverse in tranquil.

They floated on towards their homeland with pride brooding in all native hearts.

~ ~

After a few eventless days of high seas travel, thy near lands fleet was but a night away from dropping anchor, in their own shoreline. The captain was but busy, engaged in heavenly sexual incest with his beloved Ella. The princess had devoured his frivolous yet adventurous desires. She had literally driven him mad, out of the lustrous cravings of his. They were but sweating in a bond so dear. Finally the captain retreated his monstrous cock out of her gaping, eager arsehole. She let out a sigh in bliss. Wet were they, in sexual harmony. She swiftly kneeled down in front of the mighty captain and with an artistic wave of her hands, directed the captain to cum on her face.

With a heave of them fresh fairing breeze, the captain pointed his weapon of industrious lust at his beloved and creamed her face with thick cum, filled with salty yet majestic sea bound royalty.

The king on the other hand, had but already impregnated his wife-to-be, that of Princess Maria. He withdrew his notorious dick out of her divine, warm crotch, with the last drop of royal yet dictated cum falling on the side of her abdomen. His royal yet divine semen now laid in her celestial bucket of glory; and motherhood followed instantly. They were but in the hope of a predecessor, an ancestral hierarchy of the royal kind to carry the weight of legacy along and afloat.

The criminal on the other hand was in deepest of thoughts, his beau

Elta was but tired of indulging with him and his interesting attitude. Finally she stated in a confused yet investigative note, "My dear, what is it you think all day long, what but blocks you from expressing your love to me my lord?".

The old guvnor of them high seas was but in-evident for long. On the very day of the feast at the high castle, the day of victorious celebration after the conquest of them far lands, he had but disappeared. But today was the day, when finally he swooped down on to the main deck, surprised was he yet he let out a smile in irony at the empty deck, understanding that all of them sailing greats were but busy in their quarters in harmony. He slowly trotted towards his best friend's cabin and knocked on his doors in urgency with his beak.

The captain produced himself with intrigue. He was surprised to find his best friend of them high seas outside his favorite enclosure. He let out a hand in anticipation and the old guvnor adored it instantly. There was a parchment attached, intricately tied to its left foot. The captain removed the message from the old guvnor's foot and read it for answers.

It read, "Help us, my lord". He quizzically looked at the old guvnor and the mighty hiero-falcon nodded to conquer. It was but the handwriting of the, "hand of the king", the ex-minister of interior who was but bestowed upon the duty of governing them near lands.

The bosun broke his thoughts of peril. He glared at the captain, "

Ahoy dear captain, landmass ahead, we have but hit them homeland's shallows, unfortunately, My Master, My Liege, there is a raiding party in them shoreline and a ship which was but stolen from us, awaits us there, (he blinked an eye) you know what I mean Guvnor".

The entire fleet now was informed of the expectations in-land, their own ship, the one missing, bearing the conniving king of the far lands awaited their arrival with larcenous proceedings. The morning sun was dull yet it revealed the treachery below in the near land shoreline. The somber breeze now blew on in recognition unknown Them seagulls hovered on to investigate the intricate yet calamitous matter brooding in the shoreline of the near land.

--XXXXXXXXXXXXXX--

16. The Obfuscation of Reality

"Blurry vision can be due to a lack of clear understanding. At times due to shock as well. Reality is but absolute. Yet if its gravity is completely shaken by that of unprecedented incidents unforeseen, the reality is then marred by the truth. A truth so bitter yet true, it can obfuscate the reality of existence and calamity then is but inevitable".

A warm breeze blew, drawing sweat of unique nature of them royals and the returning sailors of thy near lands. The scene in them near lands shoreline was but set to disappoint them.

A huge horse-like object lay in the sands of the shoreline, a mammoth structure it was. Fifty odd hooded assassins, loyal to that of the far-lands king stood nearby. It was evident that the far lands king, along with that of the conniving prime minister, of the near lands; one who was but imprisoned, was now free and thriving in an act reeking in the epitome of a larcenous nature. The minister of the treasury was also present, smiling was he along with the far-lands thieving king.

The entire near lands fleet with fallen jaws now looked at the dramatic yet treacherous development down in their own shoreline. A hooded assassin, carrying a large white flag now progressed on towards the tip of the near lands piers, demonstrating peaceful measures.

The royals afloat now looked quizzically at each other. They looked baffled, confused at the plethora of events below, only the criminal was but unfazed. He upheld a wry smile on his face to depict an understanding of the utmost strategic nature.

The Ol' guvnor of them high seas was but in evident. The captain was angry yet speechless. The first mate and that of the second now tried to reason with him. But he waved them away. The king looked at Maria, who was in but deepest of thoughts, finally the king observed his best mate, the connoisseur of crime's smiling face. They nodded again in union and departed to the mahogany table of the captain's ship for the conversation, intricate yet of divine precedence.

" The man clad in white but was now sweating. A fever of a chronic kind had but engulfed him, the pain right off his belly grew. He swiveled around his grandiose bed, seeking answers; still in deep slumber. The angel now tried to calm him down. Finally he spoke again to continue the dreamy journey.

The master connoisseur of crime yet a divine strategist finally glared, "Your majesty, I smell a trap. This affair is but drafted to dupe us beyond doubt. The mammoth structure, them conniving souls gathered in the shoreline and the peace-seeking assassin, it's all but to lure us as bait. But fear not my lord, let us play along and gather more knowledge, let us bring in the thieving soul and hear his fake detriments of peace. Who knows he will spill necessary light into untold matters of the state of affairs here".

The king nodded and declared with uneasiness, "You are right my friend, but my worry is rather at the sight of the cunning prime minister and that of the minister of treasury rather a tragedy, those treacherous souls are free, and are now corroborating with the dastardly far lands king; then what of our noble 'hand of the king'? our sacred friend, the ex-minister of the interior?".

The criminal added in deep intrigue yet in a dejected manner, "I know naught my Lord, this sickening thought but passes me, also of the lengthy disappearance of our Ol guvnor of them high seas; I hope and pray he returns in the most opportune time to reveal the situation at hand".

They both took deep gasps of homebound air and stood to leave towards the main deck. Seagulls hovered around with a close eye on their movements. The atmosphere encompassing as well, wanted a piece of their secret talks, to make a living.

The air was salty and insidious in them near lands shoreline. The far-lands thug, the dethroned king smiled in an ironic note and looked towards the pilfering prime minister of the lands. The rascal king now queried, "What do you think, do they have an option but to deny our proposal, I know we are but outnumbered by few more than a dozen".

The prime minister smiled in a cunning yet larcenous harmony. He finally whispered, " Oh My Lord, these fools left me to die, I wanted to take revenge one day and this is the very moment, I was but waiting for, do not worry my dear king, we shall restore our ways of governance, sooner than awaited".

The air was thick in-land. Warm with intrigue and disbelief. The Ol' guvnor of them high seas was perched firmly atop them royal gates. Angry was he. Searching for answers to resolve the grave situation brewing in the near land's shoreline.

His bloodied yet prime eyes penetrated those walls of the royal's escapade. One particular development near the royal dungeon, but interested him & intrigue pushed him to inspect further into the matter. The guvnor flew into the dungeon through an open airway, unnoticed of course. He slowly progressed on and was astounded to find the few guards preparing a dead body for its final rites.

He looked closely, and found out it was but the body of the "Hand of the King". Dead was the noble soul, tortured in a filthy manner by them conspiring to dethrone the King! Dejected, he flew out of the dungeon and finally across to the near-land market area. He wanted to know more. He needed solace & satisfaction of understanding the state of unfortunate affairs in them lands.

Soon he had entered the rather busy marketplace, high-noon it was, searching for justification, was he. The mighty bird zoomed in towards a gathering troupe near a meat-stall. The guvnor landed atop the roof of the shop & stooped down to hear the chatter below.

It was but a cordial, yet excited conversation of them citizens. A few pedestrians, trying to bargain for a fresh piece of meat, were querying & rather arguing with the meat-seller. The owner glared in confidence, "My lads! The prime minister is out of prison, and so is the minister of treachery. Did I say 'treachery', rather 'treasury'! You know what I mean. I heard the royal scribe declare in the morning that our generous king and his friends have but lost their lives in an unfortunate incident in them high-seas. And that the prime minister has but announced that the far-lands king is to govern us for the glory days ahead."

One of them pedestrians stated out loud, "This is blasphemy! The cunning Prime Minister and his associate in crime have no good plans for us. Them thieves have but sided with that of the *bacchanal* king and conspired with us; I believe our mighty king and them legends are but alive."

A brief argument broke out to sort the confusion. The outcome was but always orchestrated in a blurry manner, by the conniving Prime Minister's fraudulent predicament. The Ol' messiah got the gist of it all. He smiled in a bird's way of expression & flew out into the afternoon sky.

The solo cello player was but busy playing to a non-existent, blank royal courtyard. A muse infamous, and a thick brew of an unknown quagmire, a feeling devoid of satisfaction but infused by duty.

The mighty hiero-falcon disturbed his uncanny state. And he knew finally, that his life bore a meaning of the utmost meaningful kind. The Ol' guvnor now landed near the royal swimming pool, where the elderly musician was but seated. The cello player stood & then bent his knee in respect in front of the guvnor, he shed a tear of happiness too. The great bird trotted towards him & started pecking vigorously at its own right leg. It but bore an antique parchment, a blank piece of the scroll, to be favorably exploited by the musician.

The royal musician knew the guvnor's pious yet strategic direction at once. He removed the blank scroll immediately & wrote rigorously on it. Finally, he tied it back to the great bird's leg. The Ol' guvnor hooted once in appreciation & understanding, finally, he left for his final destination.

The far lands hooded assassin, holding the white-flag. A sign of obscured peace, was but in the captain's ship now. Right in the middle of the main deck he stood, surrounded by all them brave returning souls. The king nodded at the captain to proceed with the questioning as directed. The captain acknowledged the signal &

began, "Oye ye! Tell me why ye are here, and what does this false proposition of peace symbolize?"

The assassin spoke with clarity of a conniving nature, "Dear Lord, this is but a purely peaceful proposition not a falsified one. Our great king has now captured and colonized these lands. And since you have had accomplished the same back in them far-lands, he proposes that you accept our token of gratitude & recognition of your grand feat at war; and once & for all sign, a peace treaty, not to inhabit the near-lands, but govern them far-lands only."

With a deep breath of warm sea air he gathered himself for the final part of his speech. Ultimately he added on," My lord, the entire near lands denizens and that of the citizens accept the same, so should you, Kindly accept this mammoth piece of art, designed by the crowning skilled artisans, a structure to showcase your might, dear lords, let me know on your acceptance of our kindest proposal; that is but all I carry Your Honor".

He took a bow and awaited the primal word of the mighty king. The king smiled at the criminal. Finally looking down upon the criminal he declared," Ah a noble gesture, grand artifacts to avoid war, hmmm, I accept this proposition of peace, but since the evening is upon us, I shall welcome this gift tomorrow morning in broad daylight, tell your king, I shall sign the peace treaty after meeting him in the shoreline, tomorrow at high noon".

The assassin seemed flabbergasted at such a straightforward answer by the King. He did not let out any argument, since he treasured his life, that too in circumstances like this, when he was but outnumbered inside enemy territory. He bowed and took his leave.

The evening mood was brooding. The breeze now turned eerie. Dusk engulfed the evening, the moon god's prowess of the pristine light was marred by heavy clouds. A few stars tried to twinkle and display their measly streaks of light. In the shoreline of the near land the congregation of assassins now awaited the cunning far land kings orders.

The thieving far lands king was now seated in his camp. The messenger, the assassin who had now returned from his critical assignment stood before him. The cunning Prime Minister and the minister of the treasury were seated next to the king.

Finally, the mad king broke the silence and declared, " I see, the near lands fool, their king and his friends has but accepted my proposal, the proposal of death, we have to make sure all them thirty-odd assassins of ours, who are but inhibiting the mammoth horse are but well concealed, and of course I hope the giant artifact is well loaded, up to its brim with firewood, ready to explode once its hauled up to that dastardly captain's ship, high noon it is then, the mass murder of them conniving near lands legends; once they are but sorted, the entire fleet and them foot soldiers are but hours to rejoice and cherish".

The prime minister let out a devious chuckle in acknowledgement and stated, "Aye Aye majesty, we will devour em lot tomorrow at noon, and yes the majestic horse is but made of firewood and loaded with assassins to engage once onboard the lead ship of the captain's fleet; the master artisans have crafted a historic structure, my lord, this is but a new way to win at war, we are destined to embrace home victory, your honor".

Them conspiring souls laughed out loud into the evening sky. Their act of larceny was but observed by the old guvnor who listened keenly to their words filled with malice. He was on his way back to the fleet but took a detour to understand the despicable king's falsified prophecy better. Unnoticed was the mighty bird. Well concealed near the roof of the conniving far land's king's camp. He now flew out into the night sky and disappeared.

~ ~

The captain and his legendary friends, along with their damsels were but seated in his cabin. Preparing were they, for a final debate to discuss the situation in hand. A sudden knock on his windowpane disturbed the silence before the storm. The captain opened his windows and smiled.

The Ol' guvnor trotted in and hooted in harmony.

--XXXXXXXXXXXXXXX--

17. The Establishment of Hope

"Without hope, there is but no tomorrow. Let be for a human or any living being in the face of the planet. Thoughts driven with the purity of positive hope for goodness is evangelical and often related to years of hardship and brooded with layers of faith. Once the hope of such nature becomes reality, any being mortal is but happy beyond the imaginary boundaries of satisfaction. One which is but cemented to the soul and tales told off it, for epochs ahead".

The evening had turned into night. The moon god now appeared out of the cloud cover and bestowed his blessings on them brave souls sitting in the captain's cabin. The sharp yet pristine light of the moon now penetrated through the crystal window panes into the enclosure. The captain had read out the contents of the parchment which the Ol Guvnor of them high seas carried. The discovery was grave yet necessary for them royals to decide their next course of action.

The mighty hiero-falcon hooted out loud to seek the attention of them royals. He trotted and hovered near the king. Finally he pecked on the king's hand. The right hand to be precise, multiple times. Then enacting further he dropped down flat to portray death. The king quizzically looked at the others in bewilderment. All looked confused at thy act of the Ol guvnor, except the grandmaster of strategy, the criminal.

The connoisseur of stealth and strategy smiled on, in harmony, yet the smile disappeared soon. He cleared his throat and glared out loud," Oh god, I understand what our precious friend here is trying to say My lord, the news is grave and sad beyond doubt, the "hand of the king", our good old minister of interior is but no more, he's been murdered".

The king was sad, a teardrop formed in his eyes and finally gushed down his cheek. Yet with clarity of vision for the greater good and beyond, he gracefully stated," May my good friend rest in peace, Amen, a great soul has but fallen to the treachery of those villainous souls, the prime minister, minister of treasury and the far lands *bacchanal* king; let us prepare for revenge before tomorrow beacons, I pray".

Princes Maria now spoke to help strategize their way forward," I say dear friends and legends, we divide and conquer, we make two groups out of our able hands and strike upon them mongrels with vengeance and remove them from the face of the **earth** once and for all". The royal committee of war nodded in appreciation in a united manner.

The captain was about to open his door to go out and declare the proceedings for the night, but the Ol guvnor intervened in his progress. The mighty hiero-falcon flew in and sat atop his shoulder, now hooting in urgency. The captain and the others looked at the bird quizzically. The falcon now vigorously pecked on the door hard, a notation in-turn to open the door. The captain obeyed the Ol guvnors command and opened the door of his cabin. The mighty bird flew out and finally settled at the helm of the ship near the mainmast.

The royals along with the mighty captain hurried on to the main deck to investigate the visionary falcon's primal prophecy. The bird now hooted out loud, a predatory alarm it was. He pointed with his right-wing raised towards the shoreline.

The moon gods appeared again and bestowed his light for a brief moment, concentrated on the mammoth horse-like structure in the shoreline. Even the nature gods were trying to unravel and follow the Ol guvnor's heavenly directive. The criminal glared out loud," The Ol guvnor is asking us to consider the horse like artifact which will be gifted to us tomorrow". The royals nodded in divine understanding.

The falcon now swooped down and landed on top of one of them barrels stored at the corner of the main deck. He hooted multiple times and pecked on the barrel. The captain walked towards the barrel and glared out loud," Oh lord, my friend over here is suggesting that the large horse, the gift, is but booby-trapped with firewood, it's waiting to explode once on deck".

The criminal intervened and stated," But thanks to the Ol guvnor, now we know how to cut short their livelihood and bury their attempt to challenge us". He looked at Maria and smiled. Princess Maria nodded and disappeared.

Soon two groups were formed. One lead by Maria and her sisters along with the master criminal's finest henchmen and the second, led by the mighty captain along with his able hands of the high seas. Slowly they crept in the cover of dusk towards the shoreline. One party approached in from the far left, the other form the right.

Beyond the shores of thy near lands lay a thick growth of palm vegetation. A curious event had unfolded that night, in them groves. A large group of men surrounded a man, one who was preaching them the course of action required for the night. The old cello player, the diehard loyalist of the great king of the near lands, had but gathered a troupe of able farmhands for a sacred mission.

He confidently declared, holding a torch," My dear fellowmen, we have been but duped by the far lands bacchanal king, falsehood and treachery were thrown at us, his words are but filled with blasphemy; our legends are alive, so is our great army, we shall help them great souls today with all our might". The agitated group of farmhands glared out loud," Yes we shall pounce upon them before they knew and take their life away".

The elderly musician now pointed at the Ol guvnor of them high seas, who was but sitting tight in a palm tree, adoring the progress below. He had earlier, upon the divine directive of the master criminal, delivered another parchment filled with the concourse of war to his favorite cello player.

Ultimately the master of music told the gathering in a confident note," This my friends, is the Ol guvnor of them high seas, he has delivered us the vision for our great future ahead and that of the prosperity of these lands, a "*Trojan horse*" filled with assassins and firewood lays in the shoreline, along with the thieving army of the far lands mad king; let us focus on the murderous foot-soldiers, and strike swift so that they have no chance at escape".

With a deep breath he concluded," Let us await the opportune time and the signal from our legends to initiate this act of valor, the holy war for thy glory of these lands, I pray".

A few seagulls gathered to inspect the "Trojan Horse", which was now evident due to the pristine light of the moon gods. The god *Endymion*, the lord of brightness and that of his friends, them stars, deliberately concentrated their source of direction on the mammoth structure, in order to help the brave avenging souls on the prowl.

Soon a burning arrow tore the night sky. It was but Maria, who had shot it; in the direction of the "*Trojan Horse*". Ultimately the arrow landed on its premeditated target, atop the forehead of the mammoth structure.

A humongous explosion flowed. The "*Trojan Horse*", the obfuscation of reality was but blown up into smithereens. All them thirty guerillas inhibiting it, died in a flash, even before they knew what hit them. A three-pronged attack broke out. Screaming were they, with a singular war cry devised by the *connoisseur of strategy,*" Long live thy near lands, murder em' scoundrels who pretend for peace and trade treachery".

The near lands conniving Prime Minister rushed out of his camp to assess the commotion building outside. A fire-borne arrow pierced through his neck and he fell down to his final repose. The treacherous minister of the treasury, sword drawn, evolved out of his camp too. The second mate, that of the captain's fleet, now appeared in front of him and smiled.

Finally he glared," Where were you headed my dear, your head is but mine to add to winners tally". With a quick slash of his blade, he beheaded the cunning ministers and his head fell with a thud on the pristine white sand, soiling it with a red clot of thick blood.

The cello player and his farmhands fought on bravely with them hooded guerillas of the far lands mad king. Soon the troupes lead by the captain and that of Maria also joined the in-land raiding party, in their quest for glory. Them hooded assassins were confused. They were but surrounded and soon all were slaughtered mercilessly.

There wasn't much casualty on the near lands side, except a few loyal farmhands had but embraced a gallant end; sacrificing their souls to the betterment and prosperity of their beloved kingdom. Martyrs were they, true in blood.

The far-lands bacchanal king didn't even have a chance at escape. His camp was surrounded by a dozen fine henchmen of the master criminal. He was but under "*house arrest*" in a foreign land. The Ol guvnor of them high seas flew out and sat atop the captain's left shoulder. The great messiah of the high seas adored his pet and smiled. He whispered in the mighty falcon's ears," My friend, the time is ripe, inform our king and our old friend the criminal; tell them that victory is ours".

~ ~

Two humans and a bird were in a state of divine tranquil. It was but the trio of the near lands king, the criminal and that of the Ol guvnor. The king laughed out loud and drank from his bottle of fine wine of them far lands. The master connoisseur of crime, sipped on from a glass of good port wine from the captain's hold. The mighty hiero-falcon, the Ol guvnor was in a mood brimming with elation, slightly intoxicated was he by the magic of the rum, his favorite drink of the high seas. He stood atop the mahogany table and was drinking vigorously from a bowl of rum, served by the master chef for this grand occasion. Losing his balance at times but thriving to get back for another sip with his seasoned beak.

~ ~

The high noon sun was but livid in the near-lands royal escapade. The orchestra blew on, in a brute force of musical harmony. The royal courtyard was a bliss to behold. Denizens, citizens and royals were but in arms drinking and dancing out freely for the glory of them lands. The hope of a better future was evident, happiness engulfed their mind, soul and body.

A sorry figure, was but chained to the fountain right in the center of the royal courtyard. Naked was he, beaten and tortured for his sins. The far-lands conniving king it was, crying out in repentance, but his feeble pleads and prayers for mercy fell on deaf ears. He was but ignored entirely by the souls rejoicing their resounding victory in the melodrama of the royal escapade.

The criminal was but busy adoring his beloved princess "Elta". The captain and beautiful "Ella", were engaged in a fun-filled conversation with the first mate, the second and that of the *bosun*. The king was joking with the, now crowned queen "Maria". She had been made queen in a holy ceremony overseen by the near lands royal priest and the wedding celebration was but attended by all humans in them heavenly near lands.

The old cello player was but drunk and he jumped into the royal pool, all naked. Happiness engulfed the air. Even the Ol guvnor danced on, intoxicated was it, sipping from a royal bowl gilded with gold in a utopian muse. He totted in a drunken stupor, in a circle around the king and that of the queen "Maria". The royal scribe now strode hurriedly towards the king and whispered in his ears. The king understood the message delivered and stood with his right hand raised in the air.

A notable yet divine silence followed. Finally, his majesty declared," My dear friends, we have but toiled hard and now victory is but ours we have united them three continents, them lands afar and that of ours; governance shall be delivered with prosperity and longevity of our kingdom and its humble citizens in mind, nothing was but achievable without your divine cooperation and intervention, I pray".

He took a sip of fine royal rose wine and smiled. A chuckle appeared on his blissful face, and he declared," I hereby declare that I shall put an end to treachery once and for all, so that no devil crosses our path towards glory, for moon years to come, I the king of near lands shall now execute the thieving far lands dethroned king, post which of course the grand luncheon shall continue unto the night, enjoy yourselves but excuse me for a moment".

With those words he picked his royal symbol of righteous governance, the messiah of justice and death, his royal sword. He trotted towards the thieving soul, chained to the royal fountain. Ultimately he smiled and drew out his blade from the holding. In a flash he beheaded the far-lands sorry king.

The entire plethora of royal attendance now cheered out aloud," Long live thy king, long live our dear near-lands".

~ ~

The day turned into night, the moon god now let the royals enjoy their day of grandeur by the royal pool, with his pristine heavenly light bestowed on them. They danced in merry along with the heavenly muse of the orchestra.

The king was by his dearest of friends, that of the captain and the master of strategy, the criminal. His majesty filled his glass from a large bottle of *unmixed* "gypsy wine", gifted to him earlier in the day. He passed on the bottle to the captain and glared in a happy note," My dear guvnor of them high seas, thank you for your friendship, also my dear friend, the great connoisseur of strategy and stealth, you both have but turned the tide of our shortcomings and here we are standing tall victorious, under the heavenly hood of singular governance of a divine kind, I pray, my dear criminal, I hereby gift you them far-far lands to live and prosper along with your beloved "Elta" of course, you are to be made king and governor of the lands".

With a breath of warm air he added," And you, my good admiral, you shall prosper with your love, princess "Ella" in them far-lands as the king and queen, Oh yes and since I am family now to "Maria" and her sisters, I shall be your best mate yet act as their godfather too, I will happily wed them to you two legends for the greater good and your celestial bliss of happiness., cheers my lads".

With those words he raised a toast-worthy of a legend, a glass of gypsy wine and glared out loud," By the order of thy thunder gods,

O Mighty Zeus, I raise this toast in the honor on behalf of your son "Heracles", to pay homage and seek the prosperity of our lands for many moon years ahead". He was greeted with cheers, by the royal gathering, as he downed the entire glass of wine in a single gulp. The captain and the criminal drank theirs too, finally kissing and hugging him.

A few moments later, his majesty was trotting on towards his seat by the pool, when he felt a sudden burst of acute pain erupting on the right side of his underbelly. Time froze, atmosphere too.

~ ~

"The man clad in white felt the same excruciating pain in the same region as that of his alter ego in his dream."

---------------------------------------XXXXXXXXXXXXXXX--

Epilogue

Two elegant damsels now blew out air, with the help of two large royal fans, at the man lying in the monarchical looking bedstead.

The man lying in deep repose was but clad in fine white silk. Sweating was he, out of high fever. His liver had but given out on him and an acute pain now enforced him to wake up and embrace reality.

Finally he woke up in shock yet with faltering nerves. He knew the end was near. Even in deep pain, he smiled in an angelic fashion. He had but seen, what was necessary, a utopia so great. Hope was bestowed finally, and hope so pure it was, which engulfed his body, mind and parting soul.

The royal symbol of healing, the druid, ran towards him and compelled him to drink a potion of strong yet necessary herbal medicine. A dose to revive him, but it was too late. The heavenly medication did help him to regain the last surge of primal yet herculean energy.

Enduring hard, he looked out to the gathering in front of him in his room and inspected the environment in detail. All his friends and family were there. "The Medius of Larissa", his dear friend "King

Porous" of thy lands afar, them lands extending until the "Beas", they looked on towards him in remorse.

He smiled at them thankfully. A battalion of soldiers marched on and they hailed him in glory. He could now see the strong army of his, marching by, through the large window of his royal chambers. They glared out loud, "All hail Alexander The Great!, the greatest conqueror of thy planet, the ruler of them lands, that of ours and far beyond, the ultimate messiah of our existence, under the supervision of thy heavens, may your prophecy live long, Amen".

The pain in his liver was but unbearable, yet he gathered his strength and with a feeble voice, but zeal so strong, let out a plethora of queries at his best friends. To that of "Nearchus" and his adversary yet beloved guvnor "King Porous". He stated, " O mighty "Nearchus", dear friend 'Porous', tell me is there hope of paramount patronage bestowed upon these lands and beyond, are them citizens hopeful of a remarkable future ahead, are you all happy as things lay naked and for the future course of actions?".

Both of them, Admiral 'Nearchus and heroic 'King Porous' nodded in union, tears fell from their eyes, they knew the end of a great ruler was but near, yet his prophecy will glare out loud for ages to come.

They agreed and stated in a mutual concord, "Alexander the Great, you are an immortal ruler, your tales of brevity and governance of unity of the highest kind, will echo out far and beyond unto them seas and that of lands unexplored, you shall be the colossal conqueror of this mass of land, for ages and beyond, thank you, my lord, my friend, O great legend".

Alexander now took a final breath and murmured, "O Zeus, I hope you agree with me now, the establishment of hope of a grandiose kind is but accomplished, kindly forgive me, my lord, I bid farewell, I just pray that this pure proposition for unaltered 'hope' is but embedded within all mortal souls under the umbrella of your skies for ages to come, may the strongest of all rule the world after my departure, Amen".

The body was still now, in a divine repose. The palace of " Nebuchadnezzar II", cried out loud in remorse, so did entire Babylon. "But 'hope' smiled, it smiled on, it still does".

---XXXXXXXXXXXXXX---

ABOUT THE AUTHOR

Born amidst the unblemished landscape of Assam, Abhinav Bhattacharyya, an IT professional by choice, delivers The Cauldron of Hope - a book that revolves around a past almost forgotten, yet emphasizing its significance in the modern world - the Alexander period.

Abhinav, for whom writing comes naturally, brings out the not-so-obvious elements of Alexander's later life through a historical essence. While most of the fragments connect to draw out a fictitious representation of an era, the book takes the reader through an undulating journey of glory, infamy, family and victory.

The Cauldron of Hope is his first attempt at historical fiction. Abhinav studied engineering at Cyprus International University - Nicosia, a place entwined in thick Greek and Ottoman-Turkish history. In his professional career, he has worked for Consulting Majors like Accenture, before joining Royal Dutch Shell, as a Strategy Consultant.

Presently he is the Founder of Generic Exchange (An Ardent Provider of Management Consulting, App Development and Technology Strategy).

Abhinav resides with his wife in South India. If he's not busy writing, watching Liverpool FC games, ideating, or gaming, he enjoys cooking or at least tries to pretend he does.